KISS ME LIKE YOU MEAN IT

A NOVEL

J. R. ROGUE

Cover: Concierge Literary Designs

Editor: Christina Hart of Savage Hart Book Services

Proofreading: Author Services by Julie Deaton

Epigraph poem used with permission by Marya Layth, www.maryalayth.com

ISBN-13: 978-1986097048

ISBN-10: 1986097048

For the women made of shattered glass.

*Deafness is listening to a confession
and hearing only sin.*

— Marya Layth

PROLOGUE

SMALL TENDER THING

I KNOW he is calling before the phone rings. I am free falling but I am not. I am safe in my bed next to Logan, but I feel buoyant, moveable, unsure. I jolt wide awake, bend violently at the waist. I clutch my chest but no air comes. When the darkness of my wide bedroom becomes grey, the phone rings. *Yes, I know it's him.*

I pull myself from my sheets and move across the room swiftly, trying to leave my lover sleeping. When I flip my phone over on my dresser, the screen says what I knew it would say. Connor Stratford, my husband, is calling me. My stomach lurches and my legs are waves.

I grab the phone and leave the bedroom quickly, tiptoeing down two flights of stairs to my dimly lit kitchen. The ringing stops when I take a seat on a barstool.

I want to call back, but I am frozen, still, and another small tender thing inside of me dies there in that kitchen, at 3:03 a.m. The digital clock across the room laughs at me.

On the countertop, my phone vibrates angrily. A text.

Connor: I need to see you.
Connor: It's important. It's what you're thinking.

I have been waiting for this moment for a year.

A divorce. He is ready for the divorce to finally happen.

I pushed for it when we separated but he shut down, avoided me, changed his number. I was never able to find the fight in me to push further. I just moved away. As far away as I could manage. So he could heal, and be free of my volatile shadow.

I tell myself every night it's what I want.

PART I

HUSHED AND WITHHOLDING

"Are you going back?"

"Yes." It's a breaking word, and I tell myself Logan is not meant to swallow them.

"Can't you just fax some paperwork back there or something?"

"Yes." I am honest. Always honest with him. I tell everyone he is a confessional, open book, and open heart. "But I feel like I need to go see him. After everything we did to him, he deserves a face-to-face." I don't speak of what Logan deserves.

"It's been over for a while now. This is all just legal, right? Nothing lingers?" His vulnerability is poetry. His eyes speak when he is hushed and withholding.

I reach for him, weave my fingers into his. The corner of his mouth turns up and I stretch my calves, go up on tiptoe, kiss him there. "Nothing lingers. I am yours. I can never be anything but yours." I like to say these things. It feels good to appear open.

I feel his smile on my cheek and I hope he believes me. When he pulls away, he walks to the little door beneath our stairwell.

I know what he is going for, so I busy myself with the dishes, wash my hands twice.

He returns with brown leather and worn pages clutched in his hands. I glance sideways, confirm he has my past in his palms, and stare out the kitchen window into the rain. "What's that?" I feel my chin quiver a bit, but I master it.

"Take them with you, for the plane."

"Why?" I turn to him.

I do not look at the journals.

I reach for his hip, run my thumb along the hard lines there. My mouth finds his neck and he sighs. His hands are in my hair and then I'm on the counter, wrapped around him like a vise. "I love you, I love you so fucking much."

"I know." His tongue traces my jaw. "He loves you still. He'll never stop. He'll try to take back what he thinks belongs to him. I don't blame him. I don't hate him. But he can't have you."

THE DRIVE to SEA-TAC is quiet. Logan holds my hand, brushes his fingers over my knuckles. His own are white on the steering wheel. I hate jealousy in men but this feels different. He is always so open, dripping onto pages, my skin. This hiding feels more potent. I want to comfort him but I am too lost in my own mind. I grip my journals in my lap. My eyes dart down to my left hand. I reach for my backpack in the backseat, tuck the journals away. Maybe Logan will calm if my past isn't on my lap. Probably not. My past is on the other side of this nearing plane ride.

I turn to him, study his jaw.

"I love you." I hate that I've said it here, in the stuffy car. It feels like an apology. My faithfulness has always been dodgy, Logan knows this. He was the other man. What do they say about cheaters? If they cheat with you, they'll cheat on you? Yes. That's it.

I need a drink. I hope they serve them on one of my flights. I have a layover in Dallas. I can get one there if all else fails.

Goodbyes are bitter when you have no clue what your next meeting will bring. Logan and I have never discussed getting married. It wasn't important and I have seen the way a title can rip two people apart. Expectations always tasted like copper on my tongue.

When we hit a red light, Logan puts the car into park. He kisses me and it is not desperate; it tastes like possession. I push aside remnants of past ownership. I open to him. I place my palm on the front of his throat. It's a brand, and he knows it.

"Call me when you land," he says as he pulls away. He looks down and his eyelashes are shiny in the morning light. A car honks at us and the moment is cracked.

How many men have I loved? Some briefly, some all-consuming. Some for a night, some for a second on a busy street.

The streets before us are snow covered. Plows have been busy all morning scraping, pushing aside ice, but it keeps falling from the sky. There is no music coming from the speakers of Logan's Jeep. The sound of the large tires crunching over spring's last snow drowns out the pounding in my ears. It'll be warmer in Missouri. I checked the weather every day this week, packing and unpacking.

When Logan leaves me, I linger on his retreating form. Why give me the journals? I've pushed away thoughts of Connor for months. Our last wedding anniversary passed with no thought from me. Sometimes I can't focus on that day, his presence hanging in the air like an omen.

What do you do when another year is added to your marriage but you haven't spoken to your spouse in days, months?

I would have fought harder for the divorce if I planned to remarry. Instead, I let him have what he wanted, for once. If I couldn't give in, budge even a fraction during our marriage, at least I could try to in our separation.

Why did he want to be married to someone who didn't love him back? No, that wasn't true. I loved him. But I stopped being in love with him when I couldn't be the pretty picture he wanted. I gave up and ran away. I wasn't sure where the line was, but I tiptoed over it in my sleep, as I lay in bed with him, a cavern between us.

You can only go to sleep with tear-stained pillows for so long. With an empty and aching chest. Maybe if I had given him the child he wanted, those thoughts of dying would have been drowned out by the cries of new life. I knew the truth. New life could not push away the desire to end your own. I shudder at those days as I work my shoes off, dropping them in the plastic bin in front of me in the security check line.

I pull my phone from my back pocket and glance at it before throwing it in the bin next to my Converse. My screen lights up with a text from Connor, below it a text from Logan.

Connor: I'm scared to see you.
Logan: I'm scared.

I text them both back, ignoring the woman behind me clearing her throat as I hold up the line.

Me: I'll text you when I land.

I send it to them both. The same message. Comfort is something I still am not skilled at giving.

IT ISN'T OFTEN I am recognized in public. I'm no Stephen King.

The woman who sits next to me at the airport bar isn't familiar right away but isn't unknown to me. We run in the same circles. Attend the same book signings. I've read her work but have never spoken to her in person.

She introduces herself and I find myself shaking her hand before I can stop myself. Flesh to flesh is not something I like to do. Her eyes are dark brown pools. She reads my face and I see it reflected there.

"What are you drinking?" she asks, looking for the bartender.

"Vodka," I say, turning away from her face. I am not ready for confessions. It's too early.

"Damn girl, you don't play around." Her tone is casual.

Her words, the kind that would make any eavesdropping stranger believe we have known each other for years, make my stomach flip. I just want to be left alone. No such luck.

I'm only halfway to Missouri and already this trip is shit. I finger the frayed ends of one of my notebooks sitting next to my sweating glass. The bartender serves my new friend and walks away, leaving us alone.

"How's your heart?" Just a few words. She drops them casually.

I choke on the drink I have been holding in my mouth. "What?" I ask, recovering, red-faced.

"What's that?" She dodges, pointing to the notebook.

The blue cover is faded, much like our beginning. I haven't opened it yet. I'm afraid of the truth there, plainly laid out. I'd rather hide in my novels, my poetry. Reality is much prettier there, hidden in metaphors and man-made magic. "You really want to know?" My voice is cracked, frayed at the edge like the page I've flipped to.

"Yes." She takes a sip, eyeing my profile.

"A journal, one of many." My eyes flicker to my backpack sitting on top of my carry-on suitcase. "I'm on my way to see my husband. My estranged husband." I watch her eyes darken, a smile forms around her straw. "This is our story." My voice is low, a thunderstorm.

"Tell me more."

WHAT IS it about telling our secrets to a stranger? Why is it easier?

The eyes meeting mine are warm. I feel hesitant but safe in the telling of this story.

"Tell me how it started."

"The beginning of us? Like, the first day we met?" I stare at my hands, clenched in front of me, high like a knot.

"Sure."

"I stole him, you know. I was a thief. I was as shitty back then as I am now. A friend of mine liked him. And I wanted to do the right thing. But we both know I never do."

"I think you're being too hard on yourself."

"When you're good at something, why give it up?" I laugh but it's the only one that floats into the air around us. It sounds hollow. So I fill the space between us with the story.

2

THIEF

I HATE MYSELF SOMETIMES. *Why am I like this? I'm convinced that love should be instantaneous. Attraction, at least. I know that's foolish, but I can't stop myself. I wasn't supposed to be looking at him! Why am I thinking about him?*

Last week I was at our friend Charlie's house with Danielle so we could scope Connor out that night. Connor is her new crush. I looked like hell. I had on these old brown and orange track pants I normally saved for the house. And a grey shirt that had seen better days. My hair was in a messy bun and I had no makeup on. Like I said, I wasn't there to impress anyone. The guys were sitting in the living room drinking beer and watching TV. Beer made me gag and I didn't like to drink before 5 o'clock so I declined our friend Blane's offer of a cold one. Danielle declined too since she had to drive. Danielle never spoke to Connor while we were there. She talked loudly to our guy friends, which I knew was for Connor's benefit. I don't know why she didn't just talk to him. She said they had texted a few times, so why not talk in person? Okay, yes, who am I to talk? I am as shy as they come without a stiff drink in me. So I stayed mostly quiet. I looked Connor over. Listened to his voice. I knew Danielle would want to dissect every inch of him as soon as we got in the car. When we left, she pointed out his own car. A beautiful black muscle car. Our guy friends talked incessantly about cars, so I understood the connection then, why he was friends with our friends. I didn't think about Connor after I left, except when Danielle brought him up, which wasn't often. Her crushes often come and go. When I saw him again, I reminded myself that she saw him first. I'm not an only child, but I know I'm spoiled. When I want something, I take it. Why couldn't I just leave this one alone?

"OMG GWEN, I need to show you a picture of Connor. He is so hot. We have been talking a little and I just need to see him." That was the sentence that was bouncing around in my tipsy brain the first time Connor Stratford smiled at me. The first time he smiled and made me blush. I was pulled in, but I promise I fought a little. Or maybe I just tell myself that.

I was at Carmichael Jazz with all of my guy friends that brisk spring night, a burgundy and purple place that pulsed, a place I liked to lose memories in. Danielle, my friend with a crush on Connor, couldn't come because she was only twenty at the time.

The group that night consisted of me, Charlie, Connor, Blane, and Blane. Yes, I had two guy friends with a horrible 80's bad boy name. But I was only sleeping with one of them.

Connor was the designated driver and this was the second time I had seen him. The first being the time Danielle dragged me to a party at our friend's house so I could give my blessing on his attractiveness.

Apparently, this was a thing some girls did. I personally didn't give a shit if my friends thought the guy I liked was hot, but whatever, to each their own.

I thought he was cute, told Danielle so, and didn't put much thought into it past that until I saw him again. He wasn't blonde and reed thin like I liked. But if Danielle thought he was the cat's meow, she could go for it.

I had never heard of him and suddenly he was just there, in our group, like he had always been, infiltrating my vision.

Apparently he knew the guys from high school and was back in town, hanging out with his old friends who were my new friends, and also texting my closest female friend.

A few people in our gang were playing pool at Carmichael's that night so we met at Blane's house – the Blane I had been sort of sleeping with – and piled into Connor's car.

Blues nights were my favorite. They were downtown, and I hated my part of St. Louis. The trashy part, seedy and soiled.

Our bi-monthly blues nights meant singing, dancing, and good-natured chaos. I liked that kind of chaos. I needed that kind of chaos. It kept me from my own thoughts, my own drowning. My memory lane moments. I needed voices surrounding me, voices that sounded different than the ones in my head.

My friends were stolen friends. Friends I wasn't meant to have.

They were all people I met while with my ex-boyfriend, Avery. Avery who had dumped me last summer, stolen the light I once wore.

I wasn't supposed to get custody of these hooligans, but somehow I did. Now Avery was on the outside, and I had the buddies he grew up with. I didn't feel guilty about it but some said I should have made new friends. Friends that were my own. Which I thought was a pretty raw deal. I did not leave Avery. I did not cheat on Avery. I was not having a child with some new replacement. That was all him.

Back then I would have traded these friends for a moment with him again, gladly. I would have traded the laughter we were sharing to unsee the image of Avery and his fiancée. I would have traded the jokes we were passing back and forth to be the one with Avery's child. I would have traded anything to go back, to do things right. I was a moron back then to want those things. I know that now, but I was desperate, low, and living with a sea of doubt.

The world didn't work the way I wanted it to, and he wasn't the first man to break me for another woman but was the first man to leave me pathetically hanging on for seven months after a breakup. Hanging on despite the new life he was creating.

We were together for two years. Moved in together after six weeks of dating. Bought a house together after three months of dating. We talked about marriage. Kids. Our future. But I never got a ring.

She had a ring. And his child in her belly. I knew that was the only reason she had that 10k gaudy rock on her finger, but I still threw up in the street the day I found out.

We had only been broken up for two and a half months. The baby and the engagement had been announced together.

It wasn't the way I wanted our story to turn out, but back then I would have taken theirs as our own if I had one wish. I was a pathetic masochist, but at least I was honest.

So yeah, I needed the chaos of those nights with the guys. Everything quieted then. Everything stilled. I needed shots and skin. Someone to numb me.

I didn't know who it would be that night, but Connor's smile caught me off guard. We had only talked casually throughout the night. He would join in a conversation I was having, or I would join in on one of his. We never talked one-on-one.

I was standing against a wall in warm lighting when his eyes caught me. I had a shitty malt drink in my hand and he raised his beer to me, smiled intimately. I felt it to my toes and I smiled back, hid my mouth with the neck of the drink, and looked away.

Danielle was right. So I pulled out my phone to tell her. To encourage her to go for it. Maybe I didn't need a cheering squad behind me when I liked a guy, but whatever.

Once my text was sent, I rounded the corner to where the restrooms were. To the right was the women's and to the left was the men's. I shoved my phone in the back pocket of my jeans just as Blane came out of the restroom.

He winked as he passed me so I grabbed his arm and pulled him back. He had thin lips and a thin frame. He knew how to use his tongue and I appreciated the way it warmed my mouth.

I didn't like Blane but he was a good time. My initial pursuit of him was just an act of revenge on Avery, but past that, it was fun.

Blane didn't expect a relationship with me and I enjoyed his company. The first time we had sex, he couldn't stay hard and ended up confessing that he felt like a shitty friend for wanting to fuck me. I appreciated the fact that he didn't want to be a bad friend, but in the end, I convinced him to be. Besides, Avery gave me up. I belonged to no one.

When I made it into the restroom, I felt my phone vibrating in my back pocket. I found a stall and pulled up a message from Danielle as I sat down to piss. And she was pissed. Furious.

There were a few words misspelled in her text and that was unlike her. She was trashed at a party and my text surely had been met with blurry eyes and blurry comprehension.

Maybe I should have explained myself better. But short texts while drunk were the best way to go.

I looked over our conversation again.

Me: You're right. Connor is cute.
Danielle: I can't beleve you wuld do this to me. You're supposed to be my frend.

Do what? What was I doing?

Me: What did I do? I didn't say I liked him. I just said he was cute!

I sat on the toilet for a few minutes and stared at my phone. No little text bubbles popped up on my screen. No answer.

Someone banged on the door to my stall and I jumped. I pulled my pants up and banged on the metal door. "Calm the fuck down," I said.

I DIDN'T LOOK Connor in the eye the rest of the night, but I could sense his on me. It burned and I couldn't take the fire, so I took shots instead. The kind of fire I could tame, could control.

Later on in the night, between the band's sessions, I made-out with Blane in the alley outside, let him put his hands down my pants, pretending we weren't surrounded by people walking by. As fun as that was, it didn't work to calm the buzzing just under the surface of my skin. He wasn't the vice I needed. He wouldn't work, so I sought someone else out.

Eventually, I found what I needed in my phone and ditched all of my friends for a guy I had been using for comfort since last summer, two weeks after Avery told me to pack my things.

Connor was playing pool when I walked out into the dark. He was leaning over the table, stick in hand, one eye closed. I let myself steal that look, pretend it was mine, then snapped my eyes ahead.

He didn't hit the ball he had been aiming for, instead, stood straight, and watched me go past.

I wondered how red my cheeks were under his gaze.

I wondered if Danielle could win his affections after the way he had looked at me.

3

PAPER BEAUTY

"Was your heart open when you met your husband?"

I don't like the way she says heart. As if she thinks I have one. As if she knows me.

"No, I was so stuck on Avery. I let it taint everything. Transform me into some pathetic version of myself. I was less guarded then. Still guarded, but just, less. I let myself feel more fully. I wanted to marry Avery. To have his children. My life would have turned out so differently if we had worked out." I would have left him eventually. Just like the woman he left me for left him.

"Are you glad it didn't work out?" she asks, reading my mind.

"Yes. He would have ruined me. I'm happier with the way things ended up. That I was the one to ruin me." It's always about control. I have to have it. I need to be the creator of the chaos that consumes me, kills me slowly. "Looking back, I have no idea why I held onto Avery for so long. Well, I know why early twenties Gwen did. But the woman I am now, she would have tossed him to the side. There was a time in my life when I enjoyed arrogance, conceit, ego. On paper, it all sounds pretty sad, but I know I am not alone in that. Avery was cocky and he wanted me. There was nothing else I desired more than to be desired by men. If I saw him now, I would laugh. He's still beautiful, of that I have no doubt. But it's paper beauty. I've seen what his soul looks like inside, and it's an ugly that is unlike mine. Maybe that's my own conceit talking, but I feel no shame saying I am too good for him. I was then. And I am now."

4

BLOOD RED LIFE

THIS SHITTY TRAILER is not my home. I can't make it feel warm. I hang pictures, light candles, fill it with books. Nothing is working. My home is with Avery, but he is a fucking bastard and I still can't believe he left me for that tall skinny blonde cunt he met the night before he dumped me.

THE BREAK-UP WAS CLASSY. He told me we were done while we were entertaining a party at our house. Dozens of people saw the end of our two-year relationship come crashing down. They saw it and they turned away. They poured another beer and kept on laughing and enjoying intoxicated conversations. They fucking carried on as I froze and nearly threw up on one of their shoes.

And Avery, bright and echoing Avery, just walked away, carried on entertaining.

There had been many events in my life that fried wires in my brain. Looking back now, this was definitely one of them. How do you function after that?

I walked around our beautiful home that night, the one we had lived in for two years, the one I had decorated and cared for. I watched strangers swing their legs casually as they sat on my countertop. I saw a card game being played at my dining room table.

And I saw the love of my life through the sliding glass door, laughing with his friends. No care. No remorse.

I couldn't allow it.

I started walking around, pulling pictures off the wall. I knew I should just go lie down; my heartache mixed with all the alcohol I had consumed on the back deck was a deadly combo.

My hands moved of their own accord. I could feel eyes on me. The rubberneck fuckers who had watched my life be wrecked just moments earlier wanted to stick around to see how it would all unfold. Fine. I would give them what they wanted.

I didn't feel the breaking of flesh. Suddenly, my exterior matched my interior. Blood red life was dripping down my wrist and it stilled me as I reached for another picture frame on the wall. I twirled, rabid, looking for the item that had done it. Looking for anything to fucking blame.

No one followed me to the bathroom to help me clean up. Where were my friends? Did I even have any anymore? My friends were Avery's friends. And they had known him since childhood. Even though he just pummeled my heart, they would take his side. I just knew it. I'm glad I turned out to be wrong, with some.

After I bandaged myself up, I found myself in the kitchen. I may have imagined it but I think a few people left when they saw my crazy ass walking in.

I don't know why the forks and spoons became the victims of my torment. I reached into a drawer and grabbed something, ran my thumb over the smooth surface. It was a spoon. Closing my eyes and praying the tears away wasn't working. So I bent the spoon in my hand and felt a release inside of myself. I wanted to torch the entire fucking house. I would make sure everyone got out, the dog and cat, but I wanted mother fucking Avery inside. I wanted him to feel the pain burning my body from the inside out.

Before I knew it, a pile of bent silverware was sitting at my feet. I saw someone walk from the living room to the sliding glass door in our dining room, their eyes shuffling to the pile of folded cheap metal at my feet, never meeting my own bloodshot eyes.

Fuck 'em. Let them worship at his feet. Let them see my crazy.

I sank to the floor and hugged my knees, trying to figure out what had gone wrong.

Thursday, on my day off, we had gotten into a fight on the phone. I hung up on him and threw our cordless phone into the yard. Avery loved giving me chores on my day off, and I hated it. I felt like he was my father and I was his daughter. We were supposed to be partners, equals, lovers.

He texted me after the phone call.

Avery: I told you to never do that to me again.

He never came home. He stayed at his boss's house. His boss used to be his stepfather and still treated him like a son.

The freeze-out was jarring. We had fought plenty in the past, but nothing felt like this. I felt like I had been dropped off a tall building. Avery was cold, done with my bullshit.

He went out drinking after work on Friday, and didn't come home.

All day Saturday, he spent his time cleaning our new boat in the driveway. He would barely speak to me, but I couldn't stop loving him. I sat in the grass watching him, hoping he would drop down to the ground, and pull me to him.

It should have been obvious then, what had happened Friday night. But denial and I were best friends and she liked to coddle me. That bitch.

THE MORNING AFTER THE PARTY, the house was trashed and I woke up in the spare bedroom. Maybe I knew deep down that it was over.

I walked from room to room looking for Avery, and couldn't find him. I started to clean up. Numb.

I called Avery and it went straight to voicemail.

I cleaned some more. Someone had ripped our bathroom mirror off the wall and stuck it in our bed. The covers had not been moved.

Where did Avery sleep? My entire body shook with dread. I knew it was the end, but I lived with almost-acceptance for many months after. I lived there after he told me we were done. After I moved out. After he got her pregnant. After he fell in love again.

I was stuck, still, standing in our kitchen, where we had cooked dinner together, made love on the counter. I was still there, salt-stained, a pile of bent silverware at my feet.

I FELT some of that denial slip away the morning after our blues night. Connor's eyes flashed in my mind. I saw his hands on the pool stick. The way he walked from his car. I remembered the way he smelled.

There is little life in waiting for someone who is never coming back. So I liked to pretend. Pretending was easy, and I was good at it.

I pretended I didn't like the fact that I left my purse in Connor's car last night. I pretended it was an inconvenience to text Blane, asking for his phone number, so I could retrieve it.

Danielle texted me as I was riding home with Joe, the guy I ran off with, the guy I ditched my friends for. She apologized for getting mad at me and told me she was drunk. That she misread my text. I felt a pang of guilt because I knew I was attracted to her crush. I had to run away with another guy because I couldn't trust myself when I was drinking.

I couldn't trust myself around a guy with a smile like Connor's.

HOT TONGUE

"CONNOR DIDN'T HAVE a rich kid air about him. It wasn't obvious that he had money when I first met him. Or that his parents did. I think this was why he had an attitude toward Joe, whose wealth was apparent."

"Joe, the guy you ran away with that night to stay away from Connor?" She sips her drink. There is no judgment in her voice, but I pull it out because I want it. I want to punish myself, as always. It's familiar and I need that.

"Yes. He'll make another appearance in this story." I smile, trying to hide my shame. So many men. Too many in this story. "With Joe, you could see his money in the little details. His watch, his cuff-links, the cars he drove. Both Connor and Joe came from old money. They were more alike than Connor would care to admit. And I let him have his hate. It was born of jealousy and had nothing to do with the money, or how it was displayed. It was because of me. It was because of my ties to his family. I thought they were flimsy, easily breakable. Nothing to bat an eye over, and I would turn out to be right. But it caused bumps along the way."

The silence between us is heavy. I wait for her to fill it. When she doesn't, I let words tumble out, sloppy and ugly.

"When I tell you I am the villain, I am not being cute. I don't want to be cute. I just want to be honest about all of this." I twirl the coaster in front of me.

"Are you being honest with me?"

"As honest as I can be. I wasn't always a liar. I think it happened slowly. I wasn't prepared to handle conflict as a little girl. We ran from it, my family. We pretended it didn't exist." I hid in my room from all that was said out loud, in the kitchen, in the bedroom. From the hateful voices and the violent tones. I shook my head, pushing the thoughts away. I didn't want to talk about my child-hood. Not yet. We would get there. "My job, working for Joe's family, put me in direct contact with the one kind of human I disliked spending time with the most – older men. It was a constant battle. Suppressing gut-churning anxiety, the kind that made me sweat. Choking down a hot tongue, violent words, when some old man eyed me up and down. I never understood what it meant, not for many years. This is the life we are supposed to live, right? Women?"

She nods, her eyes encouraging me to go on.

"We bite down on our tongue, shift our eyes. Hide the shame we feel when someone old enough to be our grandfather lets it slide that we look good in our jeans. That they never made them like us in his days. I rarely dated guys my age, and it was even rarer for me to date someone older. If anything, it was someone a couple years senior. Barely countable. I liked young men. They were nonthreatening. They felt safe. Or as close to it as I was going to find."

CATCH THEIR SECRETS

I HATE MY JOB. I know that is not an original statement, but I do. I hate serving others. Helping others. Because those others are normally ungrateful, and unappreciative. What is it about old people that makes them so hateful? What is it about old men that makes them creepy? Why do they have to stare? Call me darling, sweetie, hun? They hide behind the lie that it's just because they are old-fashioned, but I think a lot of them get off on calling young girls by nicknames like that. Pet names. I'll never win employee of the month. Not with the scowl I can't keep off my face. It's becoming a permanent feature. I like that I can't hide my emotions, sometimes. Mostly it hurts me. Just like that place hurts me. I can't believe I've been there for seven years. My first real job out of high school and I'm still there. Everyone else is moving on, climbing the ladder, and I'm just standing still. A god damn loser. Will I ever get out?

"GWEN TO THE FRONT COUNTER FOR CUSTOMER ASSISTANCE!"

I dropped the ceramic duck I had been pricing and cursed behind my counter. Was it necessary to page that loud? I pushed the broken novelty item into a pile and rushed from my counter. "I'll pick that up when I get back," I called over my shoulder to my coworker who hadn't been paged. Lucky ass.

I loved working in the back of the store. Away from customers. Away from people in general. It was rare for me to find humans I liked. And very rare to find any I liked at work.

Working retail meant being a slave. *Excuse me, ma'am? Can you help me? Hey doll, little help here?* I hated it. Their voices grated on me. The needy. The disrespectful. But my job offered forty hours a week guaranteed. No layoffs. Overtime as I needed it. No hours past 8 p.m. It wasn't amazing but it wasn't complete shit.

I had taken the position right out of high school. I was always trying to leave. But when I finally found a good job to take me away, I turned it down for my new boyfriend, Avery, to stay close to his job. I was drunk on his love. An idiot.

Now, years later, here I was still holding this shitty job I had almost escaped. With no Avery. With no house in the suburbs. With none of the dreams I was promised.

I made it to the front counter and eyed the line of customers waiting to be checked out. I forced a smile and yelled, "I can take someone on this register!"

I glanced at my watch before I rang the first item up. Half an hour to go. A half hour until I could race home and get ready to drink with my friends.

Wednesday nights were the cure. The cure for the disease inside of me. 6 p.m. would roll around and I would race home. I would fix my hair, I would change into fewer clothes. I would paint my face.

Some days Danielle would pick me up. Most days Blane would. I lived on the way to Paul's, our spot.

Wednesday was wing night. Just me and the guys. Sometimes Danielle. Sometimes Lesley, my coworker, and former best friend.

Things were up in the air between us. She was the one who had introduced me to Avery. Her boyfriend was his best friend. Now, she was friends with Wendy, Avery's new fiancée, the woman he left me for. And it stung. Where was the loyalty?

I always prided myself on reading people. Unless I had a couple of drinks in my system, you wouldn't catch me talking a lot. Talking means you aren't listening. Talking means revealing and I like to let others do that. I like to catch their secrets in my palm.

I had been listening to Lesley a lot since the breakup. We were a lot alike. She didn't talk much either, but when she did, it was often to people who had no issues betraying her to me.

My best friend thought I should find new friends when Avery dumped me. She thought I should fade away. But I didn't. And I wouldn't.

I liked games and I liked to win. On the outside, it appeared I was losing the breakup game to Avery. And yeah, I really was. If you could crack open my skin, pull my insides out, you would see I was the obvious loser. But it wasn't over.

I was playing nice with Lesley. We worked together and it became necessary for both of us to patch the holes in our friendship.

But I wouldn't play nice with anyone else. I would take what I wanted.

THE DAY AFTER BLUES NIGHT, I texted Connor trying to get my purse back. It had my keys in it and I had to break into my trailer when Joe dropped me off the next morning.

He let me know he hung my belongings on Blane's doorknob, having no way to get ahold of me.

I thanked him and apologized for bailing on everyone. He said it was no big deal. I felt guilty for a while for even having his number in my phone.

But then Danielle called to tell me all about her new crush two weeks later, exactly two days ago. It wasn't Connor; he was old news now. Like I said, her infatuations were often short-lived and I was grateful this one had already flown out of her head.

I didn't ask her if she cared if I hung out with Connor. I just texted him. He was a friend of my friends and I wanted to know him better. I wanted to see him smile at me.

Besides, he had been texting me off and on since I tracked down his number. It was light conversation, and I engaged minimally, my lame version of loyalty making me mute-ish.

But now, he was fair game. I asked him to come to Paul's to hang out with us, and he said he might. I liked him more for not seeming too eager. We always wanted what we couldn't have.

FORGET MY HOME

"I SEARCHED FOR NEW CRUSHES. They were like a drug to me. Something to help me forget Avery. Connor was just supposed to be a distraction. A way to forget my home."

"Your house with Avery?"

I scrunch up my face, pinch the napkin in front of me between my thumb and index finger. "Not just that. The security. The warmth of sleeping next to him. When someone takes your home from you, you make a new one. Out of other people. In new places. Anywhere you can manage." I flip through the beginning of the notebook. The beginning of the story is a small heartbreak. Back then, I was sure it was one that would kill me. I had no idea what was in store.

"My home was gone. The only way I could see it," I tilted my head in her direction, "the physical house, was Facebook stalking Wendy. I saw her on my floor, on my carpet. I recognized the fibers. I saw her holding my dog, the one I had to leave behind. Calling her 'my girl'. Even though I was her dog mom." I would never see my dog again. I would hear of her death, old age would take her, and I would mourn her. "My new home was a trailer. My bed was a pullout couch in the middle of the living room because I couldn't afford a real bed yet. I went back to all I left behind. I returned to living like the trash they often thought I was."

"Who?"

"The kind of men I always loved."

I LOVE PLAYING

I DROVE by the Alexander trailer park every day for two weeks after my grandma told me I could rent my uncle's old trailer. I had to take the long way, but I needed to see it. I needed to pretend I was making a decision to live there. I needed to pretend it wasn't my only option. I needed to stretch out my last moments at home with Avery. Maybe I thought if I stuck around for a little while, he would change his mind. I was so pathetic last summer. I'm a little less pathetic now. Or maybe I just hide it better.

LIFE in my tiny trailer with my cat, the one Avery brought home to me two short years ago, had been an adjustment.

I was living on my own for the first time, at twenty-five. Straight out of my parents' house I moved a state away, in with my high school boyfriend. After he cheated on me, I moved in with a friend from work in the city. When I met Avery, I couldn't stand waking up every morning without him. So I jumped at the chance to share a home with him.

Here in my trailer, I didn't have Avery's rules, Avery's chores. I could watch Friends on repeat and bring home any boy I liked, but it got lonely.

Finding my tribe of friends, post Avery, was what I needed to survive. I lived for Wednesday nights at Paul's Wingstop.

It was another home I had made. With friends who gave me shit, who laughed off my own barbs.

I had never asked a boy I liked to come join me there. Blane was there, and I had gone home with him a few times, but that didn't count. I didn't like him that way. We had fun, that was it.

The first night Connor walked in, past nine, straight from work at the 24 hour bakery two blocks away, my stomach did a little flip.

He sat diagonal from me, smiled once, and then started chatting with someone else.

Though my heart was still stuck to Avery's shoe, I had been single for about seven months and I knew how to play things.

Desperation was never my style. I was not a throw-myself-at-him kind of girl.

I kept my cool. I laughed and I carried on with my friends. Okay, maybe I was putting on a bit of a show, but I liked to catch Connor's eye. They were large and brown, almost black. There was no doubt he had braces as a child. I liked his smile. It hid nothing.

His little texts, the way he smiled at the floor when I stared at him from across the table, he liked me. It was obvious, and I needed that.

We barely talked that night. He offered me a ride home and I accepted, not thinking it through. My trailer was a good twenty minutes from Paul's and I wasn't ready for him to see where I lived. I lied and told him to drop me off at my work, which wasn't far. I said my car was there. It was not. I ended up calling a cab after he pulled away.

When he dropped me off, we both said bye lowly. I liked his silence, his quiet. So many boys loved to put on a show, to strut and preen. Avery was a strutter. He was loud, in your face, cocky. I pretended to hate it when we met, calling him out on his arrogance, denying him of my affections. It's always a game. I love playing.

Connor's black to Avery's white drew me in. He had a nice-guy vibe and it made me like him more but a seed was taking root in my belly. He was a nice guy and nice guys were not my thing.

I wanted them to be my thing, like most girls did, but they bored me. I wanted to chase, I wanted the ones that pushed me away. It was pretty sad, when I thought about it, so I tried not to. My life was a fictional tale, in my head, I wrote myself in a way that I could respect. But the truth was less pretty.

When Connor's car was no longer in sight, I dropped my purse on the curb and sat down. My phone beeped and I ran my fingers through my hair down to my neck. My buzz had me warm and dizzy. I pulled my phone from the side pocket of my purse and squinted at the screen.

Connor: We should go on a date.
Me: I'm not sure that's a good idea.
Connor: Why?
Me: I still feel guilty for having your number, for talking to you. I probably shouldn't have invited you to Paul's.
Connor: Why?
Me: My friend Danielle had a thing for you pretty recently.
Connor: So? I don't have a thing for her. I never have and I never will. I have a thing for you.

I couldn't keep the heat from rushing to my cheeks, between my legs. My fingers tingled.

Me: Okay.
Connor: Next Friday. I'll pick you up at 7.

PLAY THE GAME

Connor

I'VE NEVER BELIEVED in letting friends or family dictate who you dated. And to be honest, the more I was discouraged from something, or someone, the more I wanted it. The more I wanted to see what the fuss was about. To see why I was being told to stay away. And often, when someone was pulling you from something, it was because they wanted it for themselves.

Now, none of my friends were telling me not to pursue Gwen. Not outright. But the hints were there. Guys are rarely subtle. In the short time that had passed since I met Gwen, I had mentioned her to friends.

I didn't care what anyone thought of her; I just liked to say I knew her. To say we had been talking. One date didn't equal "dating" but I saw it going there. I wanted it to.

I already knew Blane had slept with her. And I knew her ex, Avery, always a fucking prick.

I wasn't expecting to find out two other friends of mine had tumbled between the sheets with her. Even cities like St. Louis could feel like a small town sometimes.

But her past didn't matter to me. I didn't care that she had slept with a few of my high school friends. What I cared about was the fact that she obviously had a thing for morons. I hadn't considered myself a dumbass for quite a while, and she seemed to be targeting the biggest assholes I went to school with. Or maybe they were targeting her. Either way, it didn't really matter, but it made me question my strategy with her.

I liked this girl. I liked her a lot. But she seemed like she could take me or leave me. If I texted her consistently, she seemed to be half there. Maybe she was busy; I didn't know.

But if I was hard to reach, she seemed more eager to talk to me. Most humans, especially when it comes to the opposite sex, want what they can't have.

I didn't want to play games with her. I wanted her to know I was into her. That I wasn't talking to any other girls. That she had my full attention. But I could already tell that may not get me far.

My desire to win told me to play the game with her. My gut told me to just be upfront with her. Why did dating have to be such bullshit? Why couldn't we just be openly into someone without fear of scaring them off?

YOU'RE SOMETHING ELSE

AS FAR AS *first dates go, it was really nice, my date with Connor. I haven't spoken to Danielle in a while, and I know it's all my fault, but he was just a passing fancy to her. She'll get over it, I hope. Maybe Connor will be just a passing fancy for me and I've ruined a friendship over a nice smile. Time will tell I guess. I don't put too much stock in my feelings for men anymore. I don't trust myself. You hear that, self? I don't trust you. I'm fickle and forgetful. I like the boys who are mean, throw away the boys who have kind hearts. I'm twenty-five; why am I not over this shit? Maybe it's my dad. I don't remember the last time he called. But I don't call either. My mom is always on me about it. I wish she wouldn't stick up for him. He doesn't deserve it. He cheated on her. Lied to her. I don't understand the loyalty but maybe that's the best kind of loyalty. Unconditional. Mine is completely conditional. Treat me like shit and I want to write you off. We don't share blood, so why do I continue to call him Dad? He's never been a decent one. I wonder if my brother feels the same way. I don't think they talk that much either. We never text and ask "have you talked to Dad this week?" It's normally "yeah, I haven't heard from him in ages either". The hurt he does to others hurts me more than the hurt he does to me. I can guard my heart. I guard it by not speaking to him. I could tell on our date that Connor would be a good dad. It was the way he talked about his niece. I know it's a stupid thing to think about on the first date with a guy you may not end up involved with, but that's what women do. We analyze everything. We ask ourselves, "would I marry this guy?" We draw hearts around their names and fantasize. We would make beautiful children. I wanted some with Avery. But he has his own on the way now. I promised myself his name wouldn't make its way into this journal again. I think his memory is slowly killing me. I wish he would go away. Get deployed. Just move away or something.*

It's been a few days since I've seen him. Connor and I have been texting more. Little good mornings and goodnights. When his name flashes on my phone, I'm at ease. He wants to see me again, and I feel the same. We sat in front of my work for twenty minutes talking when he brought me there last weekend. I rambled on about my favorite TV show until half past 1 a.m. I remember the look on his face. I think about it sometimes when his name pops up on my phone. It's a nice face. His jawline is beautiful. When I think of his eyes, and the way they looked at me, I can convince myself that my heart isn't still mangled. I can convince myself I am a little bit whole.

I DIDN'T WANT Connor to pick me up at my place. The guys knew where I lived now, and that was fine. We had established a trust. There was no intimidation, and no desire to impress them. The knowledge that Connor came from money, something I now knew, was a tally mark for him. Some women chased money, found it to be a desirable trait in a man. I did not. It made me uneasy. Traditionally, those with money treated me like dirt. Avery didn't come from money, but his family had more than mine, and he was skilled at reminding me just how beneath him he thought I was.

I texted Connor early in the day to let him know I would meet him for our date. I picked a gas station far enough from my trailer that the scent would be thrown off. I told him my place was confusing to get to. But he didn't text back until a half hour before our date. And it was to say he would pick me up, that he knew where I lived.

I briefly considered canceling since it had taken him hours to respond. It wouldn't be the first time I canceled a date last minute. I always felt nauseous before one. I preferred to meet someone at a bar. Not this whole dance. I didn't like being picked up, being dropped off. I was already anxious about the goodnight kiss.

If I liked the guy, I kissed him. I didn't make him wait. And when I didn't like the guy, it was very obvious. I'd never been one to hide my feelings from my face. I would rather be tortured than put myself through this business. I'd rather hook up.

I thought of my front porch. The wind had blown one of my potted plants over when it was sprinkling. The wood was covered in black potting soil and tracks from the stray I fed on occasion. There was no time to run out, to clean it up, but I couldn't risk it.

Connor showed up for our date in his old muscle car. I still had no idea what it was. Classic cars were beautiful, but my knowledge of them was minimal.

I heard him coming as soon as he entered the park. My stomach lurched at the sound and the hairs on my arms stood on end. He was bringing a beautiful car into the wreck I called home. I briefly considered not answering the door. I caught my eyes in the mirror as the silly thought flashed through my mind. I needed to woman up.

I didn't let Connor come inside. I rushed out, and was halfway down my rickety steps as he opened his door. He stilled at the sight of me.

There's something thrilling about the power a woman can have over a man. I blushed at his eyes on me. His face spread into a grin and I returned one in kind. Those beautiful teeth, those large dark eyes. I loved the fact that his arms didn't have a lot of hair on them. I noticed these little things.

It was a warm spring day. His skin was pearl, glowing against his dark hair.

"You look beautiful," he said.

I liked that he was open, unafraid to give the simple compliment. "Shut up," I replied, laughing a little. I dodged him and walked to the passenger door, but he followed, beating me to it, opening it for me. I rolled my eyes but still had a smile on my face. He was too good at the nice-guy thing. It was turning me off, and I hated myself for it then. I still hate myself for it now.

My shoulders made an awkward sound against the leather of the passenger seat when I moved to buckle myself in. Connor was walking around the hood of the car, away from the sound, thankfully. I flipped the visor down to check my makeup up but found no mirror. Damn old cars.

Connor opened his door and the old frame rocked as he sat down. He turned to me before buckling in. "So what would you like to do? I had a few ideas in mind."

I stared ahead. Direct eye contact was something I avoided until I had a few drinks in me. "I don't know," I said, fiddling with the hole in my favorite jeans. "What were your ideas?"

"I was thinking dinner and then we could go ice skating."

I turned to him, eyes wide. "Ice skating?" I knew Connor was a hockey player in college. The guys had brought it up in conversation recently, and my eyes turned at any mention of him now. I had skated once in my life. I was twelve and I spent most of that miserable hour busting my ass on the ice or gripping the railing of the rink. I never again had a desire to get back on the ice. Especially in front of a hockey player.

The corner of Connor's mouth turned up as he took in my panicked expression. I felt sick to my stomach. We were still in my driveway. Still in front of my trashy trailer. I wanted to be on the way to a bar. On the way to somewhere that offered me a weapon. Alcohol was the blade that I could use to cut into this tension. A cold ice rink would leave me vulnerable, awkward.

"We can just go get a drink if you want," he offered.

We barely knew each other, but he wasn't a fool. I wondered what the guys had told him about me. I turned forward, my eyes locking on the black soil spilling out of the overturned pot on my porch. I never ran out to pick it up. "Just surprise me." My smile was less real, a little awkward. Similar to the way I would be if I didn't take a shot to shoo away these nerves.

I ENDED up getting my liquid courage. Connor could sense my uneasiness.

We quizzed each other on the drive to a restaurant in The Hill, St. Louis's Italian restaurant neighborhood. I remember the moment I let my armor down. He asked me what my favorite movie was, and I answered with The Shawshank Redemption. I had barely answered when he hit the brakes of his old Chevelle. I now knew what his car was, thanks to our twenty questions round.

"You've gotta be shittin' me. That's my favorite movie, too." He laughed; it was quiet, mostly the shaking of his shoulders, and I liked the way his skin wrinkled around his eyes.

Historically, he was the opposite of my type. If you lined up all the men I had slept with or dated, it would pull a laugh from you. They were all so similar. Tall slender blondes, with blue or green eyes. Connor was tall too, but the similarities stopped there. His hair was as dark as mine, his eyes as dark. His arms were solid, his ass in his jeans was something any warm-blooded woman could appreciate. I wondered what his legs looked like. All that time on the ice had to have made him hard and beautiful in all the best places.

At dinner, I ordered two drinks. My tongue felt loose in my mouth and my cheeks were hot, warmed by liquor and his attention. He looked me in the eye when he spoke, and I was finally finding the courage to do the same, fluent glances, but still I was getting better at it.

Under the table, as we ate dessert, he tapped his shoe against my tan wedges. It was a tiny touch, no skin involved, but I liked it. The tipsier I got, and I was a lightweight, the more I liked him. My judgment wasn't the easiest to trust, but it felt different. I had hooked up with a few guys since Avery. Nothing stuck, because I pushed it away. Connor was someone I saw myself wanting to keep around.

After Connor paid our dinner tab he reached for me, helping me out of my chair. When we exited the restaurant, my hand was still in his. It felt intimate and my mind was frantically searching for reasons to pull free. The liquor in my veins was battling my flight instincts. When we reached Connor's car he let go of my hand, oblivious to the ridiculous war inside of my skin. He opened my door for me again and I didn't roll my eyes or act like an asshole this time. I thanked him and smiled as I sat down.

When Connor got back into the car, he started it without a word. I had left it up to him to decide our next move. We drove in silence to our next destination, which thankfully, was not an ice rink. I had spied two sets of ice skates in his backseat when I got out at the restaurant earlier.

Our destination was a bar. I breathed a sigh of relief when we pulled up to neon lights. He gave in, didn't push me out of my comfort zone. Something, deep down, I wish he had been brave enough to do.

IT ONLY TOOK one more drink for me to feel completely at ease. He leaned back, his body angled to me as I talked. When his mouth wasn't smiling, his eyes were. It had been a while since I had seen that look in a man's eyes. It was a desire beyond physical.

He wasn't into art the way I was, but hearing me ramble on and on about it engaged him.

"I can't get enough of Sylvia Plath. I love being inside of her mind." It was dark, scary, an untamed forest of sadness. I was becoming more and more unbalanced in my manic mind.

"Didn't she stick her head in an oven?" He ran his thumb over his stubble, his mouth was a straight line. I was impressed that he even knew who she was. Not many men I talked to knew a damn thing about the great poets of the past.

"Yes. Over a man." Too often they pushed us to extremes, with their infidelity, lies, and their lack of empathy to our sadness, our dark holes.

I stared off, past Connor's shoulder, then shivered. My skin was on fire as he ran his fingertips over my knuckles. I pretended I couldn't feel his touch there; giving in was not on my to-do list for the night.

IF I HADN'T LIKED Connor, I would have invited him in. I would have used him. But because I wanted to see him again, the plan was to go slow. I knew I had it all backward, but that's the way I operated. If I liked a guy, I wanted to wait to have sex.

I was sure he was feeling the same; he made no move to kiss me until my left leg lifted from the passenger seat. I felt a tug then. His fingers pressed into the palm of my hand. I dropped back into the black leather seat and turned to him

His lips were soft and my fingertips grazed his jawline, so many sharp angles there. I had thin lips and his were full, the kind women paid money to have. I liked the way they felt against mine.

His hand traveled up my arm, into my hair.

We broke away. The contact brief.

As far as kisses go, it was tame, but I liked it that way. I wanted more time to explore him, down the road. I wanted to savor him.

He texted me before he left the trailer park. I was splashing cold water on my face when my phone lit up.

Connor: You're something else.

I smiled at my reflection. I had him. I had the power.

I SAW him again five days later. He walked into Paul's after 9 p.m. Blane was whispering some stupid joke into my hair. I saw something flash in Connor's eyes but he recovered quickly. I didn't want a guy I had to hide myself from. He knew who I had been with and I was tired of explaining away my desires. I didn't want Blane anymore. My attention was fully on Connor now, but the dynamics between my friend and I couldn't completely change. I would not be cold to him. Not for some guy I had been on one date with.

Still, I pushed myself from my chair and walked to Connor after a quick laugh at Blane's shitty joke.

"You came," I said, raising my margarita glass to him, motioning to the bar. "What's your poison gonna be?"

"Beer, I think. I don't know how you can drink those. The mix kills my stomach."

I usually felt like I had been run over by a train on Thursdays because of the drink, but they were effective.

Connor had a camera with him. He set it on the table and went to the bar to get a drink. I picked up the heavy piece of machinery and fiddled with the knob at the top. When he returned, I put it back on the table. "Trying to capture the world, eh?" I asked.

"Yeah." He let out a half laugh. "I don't know what I'm doing with that thing. I don't have the same skills my mother has." He told me on our date that his mother loved taking pictures.

"Maybe she could teach you?" I had always wanted to get a nice camera, to learn about photography, but I didn't have the money to spare. I wanted a nice DSLR, but Connor's old camera drew me in. I liked that the pictures that were taken with it were captured moments. Un-posed.

The world was moving so fast and would only begin to move faster. I downed my drink and glanced at his fingers, lightly tracing the side of the camera as he talked to one of the guys at the table. He always had his hands moving. I noticed that about him on our first date.

He had a low-frequency nervous energy. It was unlike mine, often loud in my ears.

11

ESCAPE ROUTES

"WHY DID you need a drink for your first date?"

I bite my lip, stare at my hands. I try not to think of what she can see on my face. "The liquor made me feel free. Or some form of it. I felt transformed. New again. I felt like I had something to say. Or, that all I have to say is finally able to come out. I am a closed door without it. I have clenched teeth and a closed heart. With a drink, I am love and touch and warmth."

"And you couldn't be that way sober?"

"I didn't know how to let it out without the warmth of a shot. The warmth of my cheeks when that first sip rolled down my throat." I pause, feeling my eyes well. She let me have the silence. "Men loved me like that. Connor was back and forth. In the beginning, like that first date, it was beautiful. But then the jealousy hit. He wanted the warmth for himself. He got the warmth sober, he didn't want me to spread it around. Spread myself around. I think some girls like when a man is jealous. It makes me see red. I don't want it. I never have. There is no peace in that conflict. The flitter of hearts. The red makes me see escape routes. Search for flights out of state, just to entertain the idea of leaving. I never understood it. The way a man's anger could twist and turn me. I don't like the raised voices. The veins in neck." I reach up and wrap my hand around my own neck. It's a comforting tic. No other hand can go there but mine. "The fear is real. It courses through me."

"Has anyone ever hurt you? Physically?"

I pause. The story changes when this truth comes out. I look like a fool, pining for my vibrant and volatile ex. "Avery threw me against a wall. He was drunk and didn't remember it the next day. I called my mother that night crying. She made me put him on the phone and he cried to her about his ex-fiancée. I was that girl. The one who couldn't leave a situation that everyone knew was hopeless."

"You loved him."

"Not just him. The safety he made me feel. That was the only night he didn't make me feel safe. So I pushed it away. Swallowed it. And, again, the liquor controlled me." I hate the next part. Over ten years have passed, and I still wear shame on my skin. "I had no driver's license due to a recent DWI and Avery was taking me to and from work. I needed him in a way I hated. I still remember the day I told my mother about the DWI. She recalled the one she got, my mother who never drank, and blamed herself. I cared more about my mother's heart than my own. I wanted to be good for her, so that she may never suffer. So that she may never fear she failed. It explained why I hid my abuse from her. I didn't want her to blame herself. I would choke down the blame for myself if it meant I could spare her."

"How long can you live your life sparing others? Is it selfless or cowardly in your eyes?"

"Both?"

We are both quiet for a moment. The air swollen.

"Did you need a drink for your second date?"

"No, just a few days before. And it was hot."

12

LIVE WIRE

THE GUYS TOLD me that Connor played hockey in college. That it was his dream to go pro. What they didn't tell me, what Connor didn't even tell me, was that his uncle owned the St. Louis Blues. I found out on our second date. If I had known before he picked me up I would have been even more nervous. I would have convinced myself even further, to a much harder degree, that I was trash, that I was beneath him. When I was ten years old, I was called trailer trash for the first time. It was on the school bus by a kid named Fisher who was a year older than me. He said I was skanky trailer trash. The insult was aimed at me and my brother and it pissed me off more that my brother heard it. I didn't want him hurt. I pulled my brother into a seat and sat down, facing forward when I heard it. There were too many cool kids in the back of the bus. I didn't stand a chance. I thought idly about asking my mom to start taking us to school but I couldn't handle the humiliation. We lived just three miles from school and it would have been easy for her to take us in, but we would have heard about it at recess. Would have been called cowards. I would take the teasing over that. So yeah, if someone had told me that Connor came from money I still would have gone on the date, but I would have worked myself up even more before it. He knew who I was and where I lived, my reputation and all that, but it would have been there, boiling under the surface, that little voice telling me I wasn't good enough. I'm so glad I hadn't known yet. Because it was a great date.

HE WAS different one night at the bar, a few days before our second date. I let him be more forward. His hand was on my thigh underneath the table. He was whispering into my hair. I let him be tender and forthcoming with me. I let him be affectionate in the open. It wasn't really my style. Affection needed to lead to sex. With someone I didn't care much about losing.

This was a guy I had just went on a date with. Someone who liked me. I was thinking maybe I deserved it. To be into a guy who was into me, too. For the right reasons. Maybe it would be more than a distraction. More than just someone to get my mind off Avery for a night. Maybe someone to help me move on. Fully. Completely.

It was a pretty far-fetched idea. But I could dream. When he brought me back to my trailer that night, I wasn't embarrassed. I drank enough to forget about the fact that I was in an expensive car with a man who wore expensive clothes. And I was wearing some cheap low-cut shirt from Walmart. Living in my uncle's shitty trailer. He really didn't seem to care where I lived or about the shitty car that I drove anyway. He was into me the way I wanted to be into him.

There was something familiar, but foreign to my idea of him, in his eyes that night. I worried he was too innocent, too kind to keep my interest. But tonight was flipped, frantic with new energy, a buzzing.

When he put his car in park, I crawled over the gearshift on top of him.

His hands were under my shirt and my skirt bunched up around my thighs. I moved around, pushing off my little boots. I found his neck, traced my tongue there. His fingers were inside of me before he even kissed me and I moaned.

This is what I wanted. I wanted to see this side of him. See if it matched up with mine. See if he liked to play the way I did.

He seemed so clean-cut. Audioslave played through the speakers of his car as he worked me up close to the edge. He wouldn't push me over. No man had been able to. But I like the ascent.

Suddenly his phone started ringing on the dash, the vibration blasted through the car and we stopped, startled, looking out the windows, and then locking eyes and laughing.

"I've been waiting for you to kiss me that way."

"What way?" I brushed a strand of hair from my sweaty forehead.

"Like you mean it," he said as he kissed me on the forehead, and then the spell was broken a little. It was such a tender act and it wasn't what I wanted.

I didn't deserve tender acts from tender men. I deserved the hell I had been living in. I untangled myself from him and fell back into my seat as he grabbed his phone. He looked at it briefly before tossing it in the backseat, then turned to me.

"Can we go out again this weekend?" he asked, reaching for my hand. He rubbed my bare ring finger.

"Yes," I replied to the window, watching my breath cloud it. "What do you want to do?"

"I really would like to take you skating," he said timidly. "I know you're scared but I promise I won't let anything bad happen to you."

I'd heard lies like that before. "Where would we skate anyway?" I asked, warming to the idea.

"I know a place." He laughed.

I wasn't sure what was so funny but I didn't press. Instead, I leaned forward and looked at my trailer, at the broken blinds in the living room. I felt a little less high from the touch of him. I was coming down.

I didn't like to linger out in front of the trailer, especially with a guy who was infatuated with me. I was afraid his feelings for me would fall away. It didn't matter how nice he was. He would start to wonder why he was infatuated with the girl who lived in a dirty trailer and worked at a department store.

A girl who had never been to college.

A girl with shitty poetry stashed under her mattress.

A girl who never thought she would amount to much.

THE NIGHT of our second date we showed up at the ice rink late, after ten. Connor walked to a plain looking door like he owned the place. He still had his car keys in his hand. He opened the door and turned to me, his eyes more predatory than they had been on our first date, more like the last night I saw him. I felt a shiver, and a blush formed, just at the base of my neck. I wanted him this way.

I didn't want to be treated like a delicate flower, like broken glass, though I was often that fragile. I needed to be treated like an object of desire. I wanted to be possessed and I wanted to possess someone. Avery had been so sure in his pursuit. I needed that again.

I walked through the door, shoving aside wants and pulls for my ex. He was lacking. I wondered where he had sold his soul. If his new wife wounded others the way he did.

I stopped just inside the door, my eyes adjusting to the dark hallway I was standing in. "How do you have a key again?" I agreed, reluctantly, to let Connor take me ice skating. I expected him to take me to a rink in town, not the St. Louis Blues Stadium.

"Don't worry about it," he said, taking my hand. He didn't sound dismissive. He sounded like a storyteller who wasn't ready to give his secrets away.

I followed him in the dark, his hand in mine, watching the ice skates slung over his shoulders sway with his gait. I loved his walk. Shoulder back, head high, the sway of his narrow hips almost like a dance.

I reached with my other hand up to my opposite shoulder, giving my center a half hug. The air was chilling; we were getting closer to the ice.

When we made it to our destination, I let out a sigh. The stadium was dark, the ice lit by a dim overhead light. Connor dropped my hand and walked into the dark. "Where are you going?" I hissed, hugging myself fully.

"Getting us some light," he called over his shoulder.

I looked down at the skates he left behind. He bought me a pair before our first date. I still remember the text, asking for my shoe size, and the way he dodged my questioning. It was a strange thing to ask a girl you were about to take on a date.

I found a bench and started to take off my boots. I squeezed my feet, covered by a double layer of socks, into the first skate. When I was done, I ran my hand up my calf. I felt like a live wire, my senses more heightened. I was being pulled apart. Being pushed closer and closer into a deeper attraction to Connor.

When my date returned, he found me staring at my skate-clad feet, creating a light show with the silver of the blade onto the short wall in front of me.

"Don't be nervous," he said, sitting down next to me with his skates in hand.

"I don't like doing things like this," I confessed, dropping the mask. I didn't like driving fast, climbing rock walls, skating across ice.

I lived my life with my feet firmly planted on the ground. My anxious heart kept me from doing things other people found thrilling. This was our second date, and traditionally, this is where I would lie, keep playing the part of the cool girl. The girl up for anything. But that wasn't me. I'd sooner drop to my knees and take him into my mouth than dance my way across the ice. I didn't think he would protest but he was on to my tricks already.

He wanted to get to know me, and I wanted to distract him, with my body, with the things I could do. It was better to show a man what you wanted to see, convince yourself it was what you wanted, than to have him root you out, then discard you.

Connor finished with his skates, then dropped to his knees in front of me, his large hands inspecting my own feet, undoing the laces.

"These aren't tight enough. You don't want your ankles to get hurt. They need to be strong and secure."

I liked watching him there, fixing my mess, his full bottom lip pulled in, secured by his teeth, in concentration. I wanted to reach out, run my hands through his dark hair, but I didn't. Instead, I wrapped my arms right around myself again.

When he was finished, he stood, his hand outstretching to me. I grasped it, let him pull my weight up. He kept his grip tight as we made our way out onto the ice. His arm was solid under my frantic pull. I pulled him close, my heart thudding. I was only 5'2". The ice below me wasn't a steep drop, but I feared falling. I feared being unbalanced.

Connor pulled my chest to his. "It's okay. I won't let you fall."

"You underestimate my ability to pull others down." There was a heaviness to my words. *I'll pull you down. I'll watch that smile leave your eyes.*

"You underestimate my ability to lift people up," he said, into my hair. God, I liked him. Why did he have to be so airy? So much like the spring on the horizon? The air around us tasted like me. Cold, biting.

"Can you imagine if we had done this on our first date." I laughed, pushing out just a bit so I could see Connor's brown eyes. He locked his forearms with mine, our hands wrapped tightly around each other's.

"It would have been great," he smiled, genuinely enjoying the sight of me off balance.

Maybe that was the appeal. This power struggle, that's all dating was, right? I wanted a drink in my hand, my fingertips grazing him lightly. There was my power. I needed it.

"Think you can stand on your own?" he arched his eyebrow and my face fell.

"I thought you said you wouldn't let me fall?"

"That's just because it was the nice-guy thing to say," he laughed. "You underestimate yourself. I know you can do it. I'm not asking you to move. Just to stand on your own, test your weight, test your movements."

I hated him a little then. I glared to show him how pissed I was, and he showed me more of his teeth. I dropped his arms in protest, willed myself not to breathe. I couldn't fall over in my act of defiance. Connor skated backward, away from me, his eyes never leaving mine. "Good. You're fine. I know you can stay on your feet."

My fists were clenched. I slowly tapped them on my hips, needing to feel my weight, my steady base, when nothing felt steady. I watched Connor skate away, it was a dance, he was walking on water, ice cold permanence. I wouldn't dare move, and here he was, skating in circles before me.

It wasn't an act of showing off, nothing to shame me, but to draw me in. I wondered who he knew, who gave him access to the rink; I didn't know the truth yet. How often did he skate? His walk was art, but seeing him on ice made me breathless. It was as if I wasn't there, he was lost to the cold, at home.

When he came back to me, I hadn't moved, his approach was from behind. He wrapped his arms around me, his fingers sliding over my clenched fists. "Show off," I muttered in a quiet reverence.

"Gotta impress you somehow. It's not easy." He skated around me, threading his fingers into mine. "I need you to move, move with me."

I grimaced, my earlobes bright red. The next hour was an excruciating dance of desire and fear. I fell once but didn't hit the ice; Connor immediately pulled me back to a standing position.

HE KISSED my hair later that night after he walked me to my door when he dropped me off at my trailer. I didn't want to fall. I felt it there, in my belly. So I built my walls up, higher.

LESS LIKE A LIE, MORE LIKE A FADE

"IT DIDN'T LAST LONG. That thrilling phase. Where we were feeling each other out. Learning each other's quirks." I barely remember those first few weeks of dating. The beginning is too marred by my words, my mistakes, and the way I maimed his heart.

"When was the first hurt?"

"Barely a month in. I told another man I loved him, while I was at a party with Connor." What a wonderful way to start a relationship. With your heart so far removed from your chest, still stuck in the fantasy of the last love you had.

"Do you still carry guilt there?"

I drum my fingers on the table, on the wood in front of me, glance at my journal. "I never think about it, but now, bringing it up, yes. He should have left me then. It was just a prelude, to all the hurt I would cause him. He should have branded me unfaithful then. He should have seen what was coming."

"What's it like to watch you pull away?" she says it like she is blind, feeling me out. As if she can't see it right now, in front of her own eyes.

I indulge her. "It's slow, less like a lie, more like a fade." Sometimes I speak in poetry. Connor was never a fan. Logan loved it. He spoke the same way. He loved the same way. In a broken way.

14

YOU ARE MINE, I AM YOURS

I'VE NEVER FUCKED up so royally in my life. I doubt I'll ever hear from Connor again, not after Saturday night. He didn't text me after he left yesterday morning. And he said we should probably cool it when he woke up in the morning. We had only been hanging out for around three weeks. It shouldn't hurt this much. He shouldn't be that hurt. I know he is though. I could tell by the way he looked at me when we were together. The way he laughed. He was the kind of guy who kept his laughs inside. He would smirk when you told him a joke. His sense of humor was so dry, so unlike mine. Mine was juvenile, idiotic. I like his humor more than mine. Maybe I am too much like a sponge. Avery's humor was crass, lazy. I had absorbed too much of him. Lost myself in his personality, so loud and colorful. He left me grey and desolate, and I let him ruin what Connor and I had started. No way am I hearing from him again. And I don't deserve to. You can't help how you feel but you can help how you act. I want to stop acting like a god damn train wreck.

SANTIAGO BAR AND GRILLE was our group's go-to destination for birthday parties. I heard the whispers in our group weeks before the night of the party. Avery had been invited.

Lesley said his name around me casually at work. As if it wasn't a knife in my gut. My semi-relationship with Connor was her green light.

Since I was sort of dating someone, I should be okay with hearing his name thrown around like confetti. I shouldn't be pissed that she was talking about her boyfriend's best friend in front of me, but I knew her. We were too alike. She was never skilled at being fake, at hiding her intent. She wanted to wound me.

I questioned our friendship more often than I would have liked, but I was stuck. Ending a friendship with a coworker was just a pain in the ass. I hated my shitty job as it was, why piss off someone who was clearly on the fast track to management? Better to grin and bear it.

I did one better. I planned the party with her. I even told Lesley what I would be wearing that night. And she showed up wearing the exact same thing. I chalked it up to the fact that she had a twin and her other half was going to college out of state. Maybe she needed that crutch. It still made my skin crawl.

Santiago's had a reserved space for parties. Lesley and I arrived an hour earlier to decorate for her boyfriend and his brother, also a twin.

Connor had to work late and would be showing up a few hours after the party had started, most likely when things were picking up. Lesley told everyone to show up at seven. A little early, in my opinion, but it was her boyfriend's shindig. I didn't protest. Instead, I started drinking.

Avery showed up with his new wife, Wendy. She was eight months pregnant, all belly and long legs, spindly arms. He picked a woman completely opposite of me. I stayed clear of them while she was there. My laughs were embarrassing, louder in decimal than normal. A little desperate.

After an hour Wendy left, and Avery was on his own. I had forgotten how loud he was. He was a damn peacock. His walk wasn't like other men's. He strutted, demanded attention.

I saw Lesley beaming at him from across the space reserved for the party. His hands waved in the air as he told his story. She reached out and touched his arm, and I had to look away. Sometimes I felt sorry for Lesley. I couldn't imagine being in a relationship with someone and wanting to fuck every other guy in sight.

The hair on the back of my neck prickled as I looked away. I felt fingertips on my elbow and turned to find Connor smiling at me. I reached for him, going up on tiptoe, wrapping my arms around his neck. "I'm so glad you're here."

"Me too." His voice was warm, inviting. The greeting wasn't normal for us. We weren't quite that familiar with each other yet, but I had two glasses of cranberry and vodka in my belly. I was warm and tingly, sadness filled my lungs like a poison. I wanted to feel good. I wanted Connor to make me feel good. When I pulled away, I looked into his eyes. His energy was nervous and it fed into mine. An evening of lies and pretending wasn't promising; we both knew what was in store. Or maybe it was just me, and I was desperate for the mirror.

"Do you need another drink?" He motioned to my hand, an empty glass clutched in my fingers.

"Yeah. Sure." I should probably slow down, but I needed a numbness. I caught his eyes again, the feeling of fret I had seen before was gone, maybe never there. I walked to the railing that separated our area from the dance floor. Everyone I knew at the party was surrounding Avery. I watched Connor's figure disappear into the crowd. The bar was packed, the hour nearly ten. I spun around and stared at my platform wedges, my legs crossed at the ankle.

I never wore skirts. A lifetime of hating my legs made me hide them. When I was twelve, a kid on the bus made fun of the fact that I wasn't shaving yet. My mom had been strict about when I was allowed to use a razor. So I started wearing pants even on the hottest days. Then I started to become curvy, a new obstacle was thrown at me. The most popular girls were tall and leggy, like Wendy.

I was 5'2". Stumpy. When Avery and I were together, we both started going to the gym one year, after the new year. Like many, we were caught up in the frenzy of fitness. I was proud of myself for sticking to our routine. One day I texted him to let him know I had lost a few pounds, dropping down to 106. He told me that was great but I still had work to do. 106 pounds and I still had work to do.

I stared down at my knees. Always something I hid, now out in clear view. I was 101 pounds now. When Avery kicked me out, I stopped eating. I dropped down to ninety-five pounds. Some part of me wondered if he would have wanted me like that. Lesley told me Wendy had confessed that Avery told her she had a schedule to stick to after the baby came. One for losing the weight. All I saw was belly and baby when I looked at her earlier. It was pretty inconvenient to feel sorry for someone you hated.

I glanced at the crowd surrounding Avery, finally reunited with the friends I had supposedly stolen from him. His eyes flickered my way, skittering across my legs, my cleavage, my red cheeks. I pushed off the railing and walked to a vacant table, out of view. I wanted his stare but burned beneath it.

Connor came back with my drink and his a few minutes later. He was smiling again. I loved the beauty of it. The simplicity of his desire for me. I rose from my seat, took my drink, kissed him. It was a brand. *You are mine, I am yours.* It was false, for show maybe, but I wanted it to be real.

15

METAPHORS AND LIES

"AND YOU COULDN'T BE his? Why wouldn't you let yourself?"

"I was a twenty-five-year-old fool. I loved drama more than anything, but I was in denial about that. I like to think that was why I lied to myself so often, and why I kept so much truth to myself. I didn't want to be the liar. I hated liars and suddenly I couldn't look at myself in the mirror. Are you truthful if the only way you can tell your truth is through poetry? I hid behind it. I would later boast of my honesty there. Honesty hidden in metaphors and lies, disguised as fiction."

"Were you honest when you drank?"

"Some version of honest. The liquor could no longer mask the fact that I didn't love myself. That I drove away the ones who did love me, for what was inside, the mangled mess. I say ones, but it was one. Connor and his undying devotion. The kind of devotion that survived on scraps. Maybe that's why some people have children. To grow someone who would love them unconditionally. But the problem with broken people pouring broken love into humans molded from their own flesh was you could see all of your lacking in their eyes. I would rather pour my love onto the page, into a bottle, into a one-night stand. I'd rather not see that reflected tragedy. Connor always told me he knew I would be a wonderful mother. I saw it, at times. The way I would cry over the small tragedies. An opossum on the side of the road, no one to mourn it, because it was vermin. I wept when animals died on screen. He told me my love for animals showed me all he needed to know about what kind of mother I would be. Humans were such vengeful, ugly things. The purity of animals moved me. How could a flawed woman like me create a human made of good things? Were we born good? Was my stepfather born good? Or was he born a monster? Who made him the way he was? Who made him with breaking hands and words like knives? Maybe this is why Connor loved me. We love our abusers, right? I made a decision that night. I broke the heart of a man who may have been falling for me, at a party. I broke his heart because I was foolish and still in love with the man who broke my heart at a party. I had become all that I once hated. All that once broke me."

16

WAVES OF REGRET

DRUNK ME WAS FUN. She laughed, she was at ease, warmer than I often let myself be. She made mistakes, too.

The crowd on the dance floor around me was sweaty, rhythmic. I clutched Connor closely, pulled him to the side, shielding myself from Avery's eyes.

"I have to tell you something," Connor said.

"What's that?" I pulled away, commanded his eyes.

"I like you."

He avoided my eyes, something rare for him. Perhaps he was afraid of what he would see rejected in my blue eyes and soul.

He continued, "I like you so much. I'm actually excited for our future. I think we have one."

Words didn't come to me. I had been sensing Connor's attachment to me. Despite only hanging out for a few weeks I could tell he really liked me. I had been hesitant, careful to seem cool, still. He was warm and I wasn't sure I wanted to be thawed just yet.

"Oh yeah?" It was a dumb response, but I didn't know what to say.

I'm excited for our future too? That would be a lie. I didn't even know if we had one.

My body was humming. The bar felt smaller than it had before. Avery had a gravitational pull and I wasn't immune to it. I wanted him still. I didn't care that he was married. That he was about to become a father. I knew I had no chance with him, but I just wanted something to hold onto. Some clue that he missed me. That he regretted letting me go. That he wished the child growing in his wife's belly was in mine instead. I knew it was sick to hope for those things. But this discarded feeling was too much. I was buckling underneath it.

We finished our dance, no more words said. My silly two-word response was not what he was looking for. After we separated, I went back to the birthday party space and watched as the twins blew out candles. Connor went to the bar and I could feel tomorrow's regret in my throat. The mania was creeping in. Vodka had opened the door.

I took a seat on the outskirts of our crowd. Lesley was ignoring me when Connor wasn't around. She hated me free, on the loose. She didn't want me near Avery. I found her glaring at me once when I was five or six feet from where he was standing. I turned away and rolled my eyes at the ceiling. I hoped Danielle would forgive me soon, warm to me. I needed another friend. I wasn't sure I deserved her forgiveness though. She would be giving Connor a better chance than I was. She wasn't hanging by an invisible thread from an ex who no longer loved her.

When the singing and candle blowing was over I walked to the edge, to the railing disconnecting us from the dance floor. I spotted Connor at the bar, talking to a friend. I couldn't socialize here without him or a drink in my hand, without a crutch. I felt an arm brush the bare skin of my back and turned to see Avery walking by me. He trailed his long fingers along the railing I was gripping. At the end he turned, walked on to the dance floor, holding my eyes. I couldn't see the green of his eyes through the distance. He didn't smile and neither did I.

"Fuck," I mouthed, feeling his eyes still on me. I scanned the room, locking in on my prey. A shot girl was making the rounds, a tray held high above her head as she made her way through the crowd. My short legs burned as I left the party and walked into the throng of sweaty bodies. I searched the pockets of my denim skirt until I found my stashed cash.

"Two please!" I shouted over the music when I found her. I made short work of the shots and tossed the empty plastic glasses into her hand.

The dance floor was black, neon, heated. I squeezed between couples, drunk men, drunk women. Avery was in the center of the crowd, chatting with some guy I didn't recognize. He caught sight of me, ended his conversation, and walked around the guy.

"What," he said flatly; it was not a question, it was a weapon.

"What do you mean *what?*" The tone of my voice was unnatural. I hadn't heard it since the Thursday before he dropped me. It was an anger I reserved just for him.

"Well, you came all the way out here to say something. That's pretty obvious."

"Nice to see you're still a dick." This was a mistake. How could I be so careless, such a masochist. I both hated and loved him.

"Nice to see you're still into that." He smiled, all teeth and wrinkles around his eyes. His mouth was too big for his face, too big for the room.

"Fuck you."

"Oh, I know you'd love to."

"Hardly."

"Then why have you been eye-fucking me all night?"

"I haven't." Lie. What a damn lie. I thought I had kept it hidden.

"How's it going with Connor?" He brought his drink to his mouth, let his eyes linger on my throat.

"Why does it matter to you?" I wanted this. His jealousy. I craved it, the burn there.

"It doesn't. That guy is a tool." That would only make me want him more. What a foolish thing to say.

"You know what, I don't know why I came out here. I have been choking on all sorts of shit I've wanted to say to you for months now. But now, with you in front of me, I don't see why. You're a condescending prick, and you'll never change." I could see it here. So plainly. When I wasn't in his presence I built him up. Made him this beautiful thing, this beautiful man, that made me happy. But he hadn't. If he had, we would have worked out. My mind and body betrayed me. It convinced me we could have made it work.

"What's that make you? You still want me."

"No, I feel sorry for Wendy." And it was true.

"You want to be Wendy, and this is boring." He scanned the crowd, looking for someone else to talk to.

"Fuck you," I repeated, wanting to slap him. He had made sure I would come find him.

"Just say what you came out here to say."

"Why do you do this to me? Why do I still want you?" I didn't know if I was asking him, or my traitorous heart. The unflinching bitch beating in my chest.

"I told you." Three words. Three damning words, so true.

"I'm still in love with you, okay! Are you happy now?! I don't want to be. Not after everything you did. After the way you humiliated me. I want it to go away but it won't. I hope you're happy with your new life, because I can't have one of my own. You stole it from me." I wouldn't let myself cry, despite the way my cells were crying out. I was so angry, so red. My neck felt flushed, scorching.

His face darkened. I saw genuine regret there. We were both quiet, thinking about the summer before.

"I'm sorry, Gwen. Seriously. I am." His voice was different. So close to the tender one he would use in bed with me. When we would talk about our days. When we would talk about our goals and hopes for our future.

He reached for my hand but I pulled away. "Don't worry about it. Just be happy with the kid you're going to have. I think you'll be a great father. I really do." I pushed into the crowd, away from him, into the waves of bodies. Away from the way his eyes felt on me. Away from the waves of regret that would pour off of me if I looked at him a second more.

17

SPINNING AND SPITTING FIRE

"DID you tell Connor what you told Avery?" She wants to catalog my lies, my omissions. I wonder if she will lose track. I have.

"No. I was so far gone. Oblivious. I hung out with guys who loved to drink to excess. I had no one to turn a side-eye at me. No one to say 'hey, maybe you should slow down'. They wouldn't judge the way I numbed myself. They just joined in. When Connor found me I wasn't crying, but I had been. My eyes were red and swollen. He didn't ask me what was wrong. He knew, or he didn't want to know. I would never find out. We would never dissect that night. He would tell me of his hurt later. Of the way he heard our friend whispering. Of the way they looked at him with pity. It couldn't have been much different from the way they looked at me the night Avery dumped me. It was an ugly circle. I was sitting in the middle of it all, wasn't I? Spinning and spitting fire."

"But he forgave you, right?" She runs her fingers over her knuckles, clears her throat.

"Yes. But not at first. Not before punishing me, when I would least expect it."

18

WARM WATER AND REGRET

THE NEXT MORNING Connor was quiet. I wasn't sure why he stayed. Probably to make sure I didn't die from choking on my own vomit in the night.

Eventually, after we had both lain there for twenty minutes in silence, pretending we didn't know the other was awake, he pulled himself from the covers of my bed and crossed the room, sliding his shoes on.

I would think about it all day: the sound of his socks being pulled onto his bare feet, the sound of him clearing his throat, the jingle of his keys as he picked them up from my desk.

I remember saying I was sorry. He just shook his head, walked over to my bed, where I sat, smelling of vodka still. He kissed me on the temple and left. I didn't hear from him for two weeks.

The guys were quiet when I brought it up over drinks. They loved Avery. They loved Connor. They loved me. But there was clearly one person among the three of us who wasn't a complete jackass. Connor.

I wondered why humans applied poison straight to their wounds, without batting an eye. I couldn't stomach healing. I rejected the sun, warmth, comfort. I wanted nothing to do with that foreign magic. It couldn't be trusted. Hurt could be trusted.

And forgiveness was an untrustworthy fellow. I forgave few. It was weakness to do so. That kind of thing can be sniffed out.

I NEARLY STEPPED on the camera the day he came back to me. To avoid crushing it, I veered to the right and took out one of my potted plants instead. I stumbled over a few profanities in my morning daze and found my footing. I knelt down to the camera and flipped over the tag attached to it. "I like the way you look at the world better."

I fought the tears threatening to ruin my makeup and took the camera inside quickly. I didn't have time to stare at it and torture myself. As usual, I was running late for work. I sped out of my trailer park and ran over all the reasons why it didn't make sense for Connor to leave me that camera when I had just pummeled his heart into two or a million pieces. I thought about texting him before I clocked in, but decided not to. What would I say? *Thanks for the camera? Sorry I'm a piece of shit? You're wonderful and I suck ass?* That would about cover it.

By lunch, I had worked myself into a manic frenzy. As soon as I made it to my locker, I pulled my phone out and texted Connor, thanking him for the camera. I wanted to ask him why he was giving it to me now. Was it a parting gift? I deserved the parting but not the gift.

My lunch was nearly over by the time Connor replied. It was two words. *You're welcome.* I didn't respond because I didn't want to look desperate. The note had been so nice, so much meaning. Then his text back was final. No room for more conversation.

I WASN'T EXPECTING him at my doorstep that night, saying his soft words, pouring out his soft heart.

"When I saw you for the first time, you had broken glass in your hands." It was the night Avery dumped me. I didn't know he had been there. "I thought you looked a little wild, a little crazy. You were falling apart but I didn't care. I was drawn to you. My life was falling apart too, but I was hiding it. It's what I always do. You let it all out that night, for everyone to see. You didn't seem to care that everyone there could see your anguish."

"I was drunk." How many times would that be the excuse, the reason, the regret?

"I didn't care. I captured that moment back then."

"How?" I was horrified at the thought. My stringy tear-soaked hair, the blood, the glass.

"That's the summer I started carrying around that old polaroid camera."

"This one?" I looked down at the relic in my hand.

"Yeah. You're the artist. It was better off in your hands. Gwen, when I saw you like that I felt less alone. I didn't say anything to you, but I thought about you the next day. I thought about how much I had been beating myself up over my knee injury. Over dropping out of college, giving up on hockey. I thought that maybe if I accepted it, or raged against the shit in my life that wasn't turning out right, I could breathe easy again. I didn't think I would ever see you again. And when I did, all I could think about was getting to know you. Finding out how you handled that heartache. And then I paid for that. For wanting to know you. Because I didn't wait long enough. For you to move on.

"I keep telling myself this is a stupid idea. I've been doing it since that night. But I can't stop thinking about you. I know you had a serious relationship with Avery and it can be hard to get over. I shouldn't just expect you to not care about him anymore. I shouldn't push and I still want to see you. Maybe this will all blow up in my face, a big part of me thinks it will, but I want to try." He reached out, took one of my hands into his, stared at them.

I didn't know what to say. I overanalyzed the meaning of the camera all day at work, finally working myself up so much I asked to leave an hour early. When I got to my trailer, I drew a hot bath and stared at the framed key on my bathroom wall. I would never find the key to this life. To the way we hurt and ran from each other.

I had just pulled myself from my bath, was dripping warm water and regret onto my rug, when Connor knocked on my trailer door. His heavy fist rattled the rusty metal, sending my heart into a thunderous race.

I was sitting on the edge of my bed when his speech finished. I looked at his knuckles. They were worn, just slightly. The skin on his hands was so smooth, with little hair dusting it.

"So you want to keep going with this?" I asked, tentatively, focusing on the way his thumb lightly trailed my palm.

"Yes. I do. If you're still in it."

"I am. I just, I know I screwed it up. And when I saw the camera I didn't know what it meant to you."

"I didn't know what it meant this morning when I left it, really. I've been thinking about you all day. About us. About this. I've been angry and sad and just confused as hell but when it comes down to it, I want to be with you. I don't want to let my pride take that away from me. I've done that before in the past and I won't make that mistake again."

I thought of all the things my pride had taken from me. What a vengeful thief it could be.

I stood up, let Connor wrap his arms around me. I worked over our conversation. Looked for the catch, the fine print, the trap. I didn't find anything then, but I would soon. Sometimes our intentions are pure, but there is a little animal inside of us who won't let hurts lie and die. That animal will dig everything up – corpse and bone and poison. That animal will not let us live, move on, without seeing the remains of all we have done.

CONNOR STAYED THE NIGHT. We took turns touching each other. I could feel his restraint. His almost forgiveness, so much paler than his words, paler than his intentions.

I offered my best parts to him. What I had learned were my best parts, and he chose to hold me instead. To save me from regret. He didn't know me well enough to know I no longer held regret on my tongue. I swallowed it down and forgave my flesh for what I willingly gave up.

19

BATHE ME IN SALT

"PRIDE IS A POWERFUL THING. What he once said wouldn't get in our way, ended up tearing us apart. Or maybe that's a lie I want to tell myself. To make him the shining knight. I can't tell you he was always perfect, always pure. That would be a lie."

"But," she laughs, reaches out to touch my hand, "you said you lie a lot. And there seems to be so many here."

"I won't lie about this. Connor was flawed, too. He didn't deserve all I put him through, but he wasn't innocent. And I would soon learn that. I think, when he first met me, he looked at me with rose-colored glasses. He didn't see the cracks. After I hurt him, he took them off. He saw all that I was then. He saw my life, how it compared to his. It couldn't measure up."

"You always say he had a perfect life. What do you mean?"

"His parents were still together. Mine had ended their relationship before I could speak. My biological father stole TVs to support his drug addiction, left town before I could say the word 'Daddy'. My mother and I had a similar heart, had been hurt the same way, by some of the same men. Patterns repeat all too often in this world. The sad kind. I know more women who have had no father, who have been raped, who have been beaten, than those who live happy full lives with no scars littering the past, their skin. I like likeness in women. I like our sadness, so close to a mirror.

"I couldn't relate to the kind of women who smiled all the time. Maybe that's why I didn't understand why Connor chose me. His mother and sisters, I would eventually learn, were smilers, laughers, happy women. I didn't know their past and I didn't know if they had ever been broken like me, but if they had, they didn't wear it the way I did. Maybe that's what was wrong with me. I couldn't swallow and camouflage my aches the way they could. I wasn't a good actress. It was a good thing I gave up that dream when I was seven years old. I stopped wanting to go on stages at that age. It was the same age I learned that a father's hands are not always cleaning cuts, mending wounds. But instead, creating the kind that never go away. The kind you can't recover from." I can't help the tears that are welling up. I turn to poetry, to hide. "Bathe me in salt. Help me heal this." I'm not speaking to anyone. Just out loud, to myself. "Why do so many turn to god? Would he fix me?" I don't wait for an answer. "I wish I could believe in him, but I can't. I can't rely on a book that says a man can do what my stepfather did to me and ask for forgiveness and then gain access to heaven and the ever-after. A book that says if I kill myself today because of all he did, I would burn in the hell beneath my feet. No. I won't swallow that lie. I'd rather choke on my own."

20

CHEAP

Connor

DECIDING to date Gwen again wasn't a lie. It was what I wanted. But I couldn't get over the way she wanted other men. She told me she wanted me, but I worried even she had no clue what she wanted.

I pulled away after her drunken confession to Avery. And now, she wanted me and it all felt cheap. I felt like something on a check list. Would she have even desired me if I hadn't shown her I was tired of the drama?

And my god, the girl was drama. She was the kind that complained about everyone else who had drama in their lives and said she wasn't into it. But she was. And we all knew it.

Despite everything inside of me telling me she was bad news, to just cut ties, I was making some regretful commitment to her. There was something in the pit of my stomach, some hopeful hanging on. Hopeful that she would change now that we were trying again, but I wondered how committed she would be to a relationship with a guy who clearly did not forgive her.

You can't help how you feel. None of us could. It was her actions that bit, her lack of words. She wanted me to know she was changed; I saw it in her eyes, but that's all I got. Hopeful looks. Can you survive on that? Doubtful.

I was humiliated at the twin's birthday party. I could bury a lot, but this nagging regret kept surfacing. I felt like I spent half of my time with Gwen holding her hand and the other half holding a shovel for all the shit I wanted to say.

I wanted to try again, but my heart wasn't letting me.

21

TO BE CHOSEN

AT FIRST, *everything was great. I had a great past few weeks with Connor. But now he seems distracted, strange. It wasn't a sudden drop in behavior. It has been a quiet drift, now that I think about it. Now that I look back at his actions. He has been pulling away slowly. I think he regrets his decision to forgive me. Maybe he isn't as strong as he thought. Maybe people are giving him shit for letting me back into his life. No one wants to be that guy. He said he wouldn't let his pride get in the way. But I think it's winning. And then there is the thing I don't want to think about. Blane told me that Penny girl has been visiting Connor at work. They've been friends since high school. And she has a boyfriend. But that doesn't put me at ease. If she has a boyfriend, why isn't she visiting her boyfriend at work? Why is she visiting Connor? They've been together a long time. I'm sure she is feeling that boredom. She wants to indulge a crush. One of the guys works with Connor and he says Penny will sometimes be there for an hour, chatting it up with Connor, laughing with him. I'm too scared to bring it up to Connor. What can I say? I can't bring up the reason I hate her to begin with. Avery is a name I will never bring up again. The wound is too fresh. This feeling in my gut, I wish it would go away. I wish she would go the fuck away, too.*

PENNY, like a bad penny, always turned up. Avery lost his virginity to her. Then, lovely plot twist, Connor had sex with her in high school, too. I really needed to expand my circle beyond these boys who all graduated together. It was becoming an issue.

I don't know why women hate other women who are different from them so much. Maybe it was due to the fact that society was always training us to be carbon copies of one another. Girl-on-girl hate was ingrained in us when really, we needed to stick together.

Penny was a tiny thing. Lean, slender. She didn't have the curves I did, the ones I had been self-conscious of since I was twelve years old. She had red hair down to the middle of her back, and she wouldn't be the first redhead to catch Connor's eye. He loved them, and I, in turn, learned to loathe them. I tried to push thoughts of her away.

I DIDN'T GO to high school in the city. I was a small-town girl and I moved to the metro area after graduating. I loved my small-town upbringing, but it wasn't where I wanted to spend my life. At times, I craved a return to the quiet of it all. I missed the stars; they spoke to you when no one else would.

I had been invited to a party with some old classmates on Saturday night. Connor agreed to go with me. I felt a thrill, knowing it would be our first time hanging out with other people since he decided to forgive me for the party. I didn't deserve it. I had humiliated him, and I was too drunk to see it.

I thought of my stepfather. It had been months, maybe a year, since I last heard from him.

The party was close to where I grew up, where he lived from time to time. His work kept him in Kansas City most of the time. I never knew how his family life was going. He always boasted of his wife, his stepchildren. The replacements.

My mother encouraged me to reach out to him more often than I would have liked. If you're not reaching out, then you're not setting yourself up for the freeze-out. I didn't know how often my brother talked to him. My stepfather, my brother's biological father, was a stale topic to bring up. It left a bad taste in our mouths. Abandonment and something I couldn't put a finger on. It was best not to try. I didn't know yet.

On the way out to the party, Connor was still off, still drifting away from me. He told me about his day, his week. He reached for my hand twice, but let it go quickly. It felt like a reflex, then a burn. A touch he desired but was stung by. It was expected. Maybe he wasn't as good with forgiveness as I hoped, maybe he was more like me than I could handle.

The house was in the woods, down a long driveway. I drove, hoping Connor could have a few beers, relax. I wanted him to have fun, and just being in his presence again, after what I did, that was enough for me.

I thought being in the presence of people I grew up with would put me at ease. I was always with the same guys, this group of friends who had known each other since kindergarten. I wanted to be with my people, even though I could hardly call them that. I hadn't kept in touch with anyone from my adolescence, but I had a history with them. Maybe they could paint me in a better light than I was painting myself in.

We were only at the party for an hour before I wanted to leave. Connor smiled as I introduced him to people. He shook hands and laughed. But to me, he was gone, cold and aloof. He was constantly looking at his phone. And when he would look at his phone, he would smile. The corner of his mouth would turn up. He hadn't smiled at me like that since before. I wanted to hate him. And part of me did. But the bigger part hated myself. I did this. I sabotaged this.

"Are you having fun?" I would ask.

"Yes. You asked me that twenty minutes ago. The answer hasn't changed."

I didn't like this version of him, tight and cold.

Before long, I told Connor I wanted to leave, not wanting to subject myself to any more of our pathetic act. We drove back to the city in silence. He had the decency to put his phone away. I could hear it buzzing in his pocket. The red in me bubbled up, threatening to spill over. I wanted to jerk the car to the side of the road, walk into the black, and scream. But I didn't. I let my white knuckles speak for me. I let the heavy sound of my breathing, my blind anger, speak.

When we got back to my trailer, I put my car in park and jumped out, walking for my door. I heard the passenger door close as I made it up my steps. I stopped, my key in the door, when Connor spoke.

"I'm sorry. It was a mistake to ask you back. That's on me. You're not wrong there. And I know when you and I started back up again you had great intentions. I'm the asshole here. I thought I would let it go, but I can't. I want to be chosen. I don't want to be someone's second choice. The consolation prize. That's all I really am. If Avery left his wife and wanted you back, you would go, I know you would and I don't even want you to respond to that comment. We both know it's true. I deserve better and you, you deserve better, too. I'm not giving you all of me. I wanted to, I swear I did. But I can't stop thinking about that night. About the way everyone felt sorry for me and the way they looked at me."

I pulled the key out, turned, staring at my shoes. I heard a car alarm go off in the distance, followed by yelling.

"So you're letting your pride win?" I looked at him. He was leaning against the side of his car, his arms crossed at his broad chest.

"I guess I am. But at least I'm admitting it now, and not dragging it on. Three weeks was too long."

"Long enough to get my hopes up." To get me to bed. To fake it enough that I changed my view. That I wanted him. Long enough to break my heart over that red-headed tramp. Neither of us were saying her name, but I knew she was the reason for this. She was showing interest and he was being pulled in. He didn't want to be with a girl who was still a little in love with her ex, but he wanted to give his time to a girl who was in an actual relationship with another guy? Fuck him. Fuck this shit. Again, I saw red. Not red like that bitch's hair, red like the rage thundering up again. I looked down at the keys in my hands. Imagined throwing them across the driveway. "Go home," I said, flatly.

He didn't argue, just said "okay" and had the audacity to sound a little sad. His phone went off in his pocket again and I wanted to run down the steps, lunge for it, pull it up, and see her name. Show it to him.

I wanted to stop dancing around the reason. The real one for this bullshit.

I WATCHED his car drive away from my trailer, then stood frozen on my steps. Eventually, I went inside and texted Blane. He was at the bar. I didn't even have to ask. Before we got off the phone, he told me a cab was coming to get me.

The drive there was static with my wrath. I was plotting my revenge. A dozen scenarios played out in my head. Fuck Connor. I wanted out of this game. No, I was going to win this game.

PART II

22

NOTHING MORE THAN MY SKIN

"WHEN YOU'RE LIVING your life aimlessly you avoid it, the truth of it all. I did that for a very long time. I also avoided the fact that I let the men in my life determine where I was going."

"What do you mean?"

"After high school, I skipped college to hang around my boyfriend so he wouldn't cheat on me. I didn't trust him. He cheated on me five days after I lost my virginity to him. And I stayed. It doesn't get much dumber than that. I stayed at my shitty job to be close to Avery. I was stuck in a career that I didn't want to be in. And a trailer I didn't want to be in. Because my home had been ripped from me. It was easy to pine for the white picket fence life when your childhood wasn't safe, secure. More than anything, I just wanted to be taken care of in those days. Later, I would reject it. And then I fell into the phase where I didn't want to give up my freedom, I'm still not sure I'll ever leave that phase. It was hard to find a balance. I wanted to give things up and I wanted to hold things close. I was settling into a routine of solitude. I lived alone for five years. I started to like coming home to an empty house. Just my cat and my dog. I went for walks. I went to the gym. I did it all alone and I loved that. I wanted to go to Walmart alone. I wanted to go to the mall alone. I wanted to do everything alone and it didn't feel lonely as long as I had someone temporary to warm my bed. After Connor and I ended our brief romance, I found so many replacements. It would be a messy two years. And Connor and I would see each other again. So many times. I would learn, over and over again, that he was exactly the kind of man I craved. The kind I had wished he was in the beginning, because it was something I could understand. Something I was used to."

"And what were you used to?"

"Being used for nothing more than my skin."

23

SUCH A DOWNER

I've been avoiding everyone. Finding solace in words, in reading. In movies on repeat. I watched The Shawshank Redemption twice today while I was off work. I can't afford cable, so this is what I'm stuck doing. A girl at work begged me to buddy read Twilight with her. So I did. I can see why people thought it was fun. I like random obsessions. So now I am reading every vampire novel I can get my hands on. I've been avoiding the bar, my friends. My phone keeps lighting up and sometimes I turn it off. I want everyone to leave me alone but I know as soon as they do, as soon as my phone stops beeping, I'll miss everyone. I'll come out of hiding then. It's nice to be wanted. To know I am missed. That wing night isn't the same without me. But I need a reset.

I'M NOT sure what to do with myself most days. I bounce between cowering and crawling out of my hole. I'm no longer hiding in my trailer every day. I've been spending Sundays on the water with the guys. Connor doesn't come around. I've stolen friends from another guy. I want to feel bad, but they both ended it with me, so I have a hard time finding the pity. I tried to find comfort in Blane, but it was no longer fun. We even tried to go on a date last week but it was obvious from the moment he picked me up that we were nothing more than friends.

My thin friendship with Lesley has been bouncing and wobbling. At first, she seemed thrilled that Connor was done with me, then she flipped, realized I was on the loose again. Free to fuck every guy she had a crush on that wasn't her boyfriend. At times, it's tempting to just date Blane to get under her skin. I heard the story of the time she stripped to her underwear in front of him while her boyfriend was passed out, begging Blane to touch her. I loved the guy, his morals lacked in a lot of areas, and then in others, he showed surprising restraint. He said he didn't touch her.

No one brings Connor up in my presence. Which is a relief. My grief, to them, is strange. They walked me out of the pit Avery had left me in. But it was expected, with all we shared. Connor and I had barely dated so I think it was all confusing to them. It was confusing to me.

"Dude, I didn't expect you to be this sad," Blane said one night in his car, after wing night, in my driveway.

"I know," I groaned, leaning back in the passenger seat. "I don't even know why I still care. We barely dated, right?"

"You and I are just alike. We want what we can't have. You're such a guy."

I punched him in the arm. "It's why we could never date. We are too alike, I agree. And maybe you're too much of a girl?"

"Same difference." He drummed the steering wheel. "Snap out of it, buddy. I miss the old Gwen. She's much more fun than this."

"Sorry my broken heart is such a downer." I wasn't mad, I liked this teasing. I felt more normal.

Was he right? Was it because he didn't want me anymore? Was that the reason for this want I had for Connor? Did it grow from rejection? I was a magician, I guess. Turning simple wants into star-crossed despair.

This felt different, though. In the end, I saw some light, it shined on a simple future.

One I knew we could share together. If I hadn't gotten in our way.

His decision was so final. I saw a little bit of the warning I had been fed by strangers. That he wasn't a nice guy. I knew they were wrong, but he wasn't as innocent as I feared. He could break hearts just like the rest.

24

WORDS CHOKED IN THROATS

"WHEN DID YOU SEE CONNOR AGAIN?"

I laugh. It would be so simple if anything we did made sense. "He didn't give me a chance to move on from our short thing. He texted me, asking to come by. It got my hopes up. But it turned out to just be sex. And it was great sex, better than anything that happened between us when we were dating. It felt like we were no longer concerned with impressing each other. There was no pressure. Our chemistry when we were skin-to-skin was thrilling. And it pulled me. I don't care what anyone says, you can't have sex with someone without at least one of you falling."

"And it was you?"

"Yes. I was finally falling for him. Because I knew then, with certainty, that I could no longer have him. We carried on that way for the rest of the summer. When September rolled around, we were still meeting up every week. Still fucking desperately. I thought maybe I could turn it into more. So I worked overtime for weeks to save up some extra cash. I bought us Cardinals baseball tickets and set up a nice weekend at a hotel. I didn't want to stay in my trailer or his sister's house, where he was living."

"So it was a gesture, of sorts."

"Yes. Looking back at it now, I know I knew he didn't want to be with me. I led us here, to this falsehood and words choked in throats. Once, he couldn't get enough of me. He blushed when he brought up his hope for our future. Now, we met in the night, after everyone else was asleep. When he could be sure no one knew my car was pulling into his driveway. He lied and I lied and I let myself believe it was what I wanted. It was my punishment for breaking his heart. I thought if I did my time he would change his mind about me, about us. It was silly to think that one day he would wake up and magically decide to make a girlfriend out of the girl who was giving her body to him freely. He was showing me what he wanted from me, and what he didn't need anymore. I was showing him how desperate I was, how little pride I had left. And now I thought, somehow, if I bought him a birthday present, something a girlfriend would get a guy, he would turn me into what I wanted to be. Just, his."

"And he didn't."

"No, he didn't. He turned someone else into his."

25

FORCED SUFFERING

I CAN'T STAND the sight of her face. It's round like a pumpkin. In the picture I saw on Facebook, Connor had his arm draped over her shoulder. They were both smiling. Her teeth looked like little chiclets. Candy corn asses. She tans too much. Her brown hair fades into her fake brown face. Her shoulders are boxy and I fucking hate her. I have no pictures with Connor like the one I am staring at now. We never made it to a holiday. We started hanging out after Valentine's Day, we were done, officially, before summer started. Now here she was...five years younger than me, sharing pictures of their first Thanksgiving together. I was spending Thanksgiving alone. The same as last year. I found some pictures of Connor and I. Lesley took them at the bar. They are candid. We didn't pose. In one I am whispering something in his ear, and the look on his face makes me ache. He really cared about me. I can see it there, in that moment, captured forever. I didn't know what I was telling him in the picture. Some secret about one of our friends maybe. I wish I had appreciated him. I think my heart is going to burst out of my chest sometimes. When I saw pictures of Avery and his new wife, the woman he left me for, it didn't hurt like this. I was with him for two years and I am more numb, more desolate over a guy I was never officially in a relationship with. Time really is irrelevant. The rules are bendy and bullshit. I just want the image of their faces to go away. I want all this hurt to go away.

I LOOKED down at the single bowl of mashed potatoes in my hand, at the pathetic single tear on my thumb.

The bowl fell in slow motion, a dramatic descent to my cheap, ripped, linoleum floor. My dog Holly hopped up from her bed and ran to lap up the contents. I couldn't tear my eyes from my laptop on the dining room table. A Charlie Brown Thanksgiving played softly in the background.

I deactivated my Facebook. I couldn't look at Connor and pumpkin-faced-Tracey anymore. I would end up leaving it deactivated for a year.

THE REST of the holidays went by slowly, achingly brutal. I spent most of the hours I wasn't working in my bedroom of my tiny trailer watching Friends and Buffy reruns. I took on extra hours at work. My car broke down twice and I had to take the bus for a while.

Blane, who I no longer slept with since we lost interest in each other's skin, would pick me up for the bar on Wednesdays so I never had to miss out.

I flipped through them. Men. Men with hands like a salve.

First, there was Jesse, he was twenty, and I met him online. We slept together twice, so I never counted it as a one-night stand. Eventually, I ghosted him.

The next guy was the reason I stopped meeting guys online. I had to kick him out of my trailer after a frightening hour on my couch of heavy petting and no's that were repeated too many times.

Sex had become a weapon. Men and women wielded it in such strange ways. I just wanted someone to crave me beyond flesh. I wasn't sure what I would do with someone like that, they weren't Connor, and I felt foolish for holding onto my desire for him. We had such a short time together. I was fixated on the idea of him as a partner. The white picket fence life.

I had a tiny chain link fence behind my trailer. It was rusty, one side was held together by some zip ties I bought at Walmart. I worked with my hands all day at work. When I got off, I didn't want to move. I wanted to lie in bed, relax.

There was no one to help with the things that were falling apart at home. Did I find Band-Aid fixes for everything? My trailer had three bedrooms. One was full of everything personal my uncle owned. It was a storage shed for all the things he wanted when he got out of prison. There was a large tool chest in there and sometimes I would rifle through it looking for nails, a hammer.

ALL THINGS eventually come to an end, right? The year, the shitty year, would finally bleed away. 2009 promised something better. They all did. We stepped into January hoping everything would be different.

I promised myself I would be different. No more fucking nameless, faceless nobodies. No more texting Connor; he never answered anyway. And that made me want him even more. Knowing that if he was with me, he would ignore another girl's texts. It's such a silly thing. His faithfulness to Tracey, the way he pretends I didn't exist, still pulled me to him.

But I promised myself I would let him go in the new year. I would find a distraction that was more permanent. More than just fucking. But skin and liquor were the only things pulling me out of my hole, one that was sinking deeper and deeper beneath my feet.

Sometimes an unnamed grief took over. Something gnawing, something I couldn't pinpoint.

That's where I was at then. It was a different time, we didn't talk about those things, and I didn't know anyone who suffered from any sort of mental illness. It seemed like such a damning phrase then. Mentally ill. I wasn't certifiable. I thought idly about killing myself, from time to time, but in that not-so-serious way.

When things would pile and push I would think that tomorrow was something I did not want to see. I never thought of actually ending it. I didn't want to die, but I didn't want to be alive. I had my dog and my cat to feed. They relied on me. Sometimes it felt like they were the only ones who needed me. They truly relied on me, in the way that simple friendships and casual hookups could never compare to.

I think having someone really rely on me would be too much. How would I fare as a mother? It wasn't something I thought about too often at that point. I couldn't even keep a boyfriend. Should you have children if you shy away from hugging? Skin-to-skin touch that is not sexual? Sometimes when I was drunk I liked to hang on my friends, hug them. That was about it though. No funny hand holding or friendly kisses on cheeks. I liked to hug. Only then though. A sober hug was an act of intimacy I didn't want, nearly as scary as hand-holding.

The odd thing about being someone who proclaims themselves as someone who doesn't like a hug, is that more people want to hug you. They want to pry one from you. They want to feel special, to say "she doesn't like hugs but she lets me hug her". I didn't understand it. Why would you want to purposely make someone feel uncomfortable? It made me resent people. I wonder when it stopped, my giving away of hugs. Was I a child that loved hugs? Did I stop at some point, for some reason? I'd seen videos of myself when I was five years old. I talked and talked and I was loud, happy, boisterous. When I was a teenager, things changed. But aren't most teens supposed to be moody?

I didn't want to be hugged. I hated being caught in a bathing suit. I was very curvy, voluptuous. I didn't want grown men, especially anyone in a father type position, to look at me.

It was strange to have something so spelled out for you, and to not see it. Denial is a powerful drug. I ached for every little girl who was forced to hug her creepy uncle. To sit on a stranger's lap because he was dressed as Santa Clause. My mother showed me pictures of myself with Santa. I was always screaming, in pure terror. Why was I forced to try again every year? Traditions are hard to break away from. We are all victims of "this is what you're supposed to do" guilt.

I wouldn't force these things on my child if I had one. No forced affections, no forced feelings.

Imagine a little girl being in control of her own little body. I wish I had known what that was like.

I wonder what childhood will be like for little girls, hundreds of years from now. If we will finally be where we need to be.

I believed in reincarnation. I believed I would see it one day, those horrors far behind me.

I was once obsessed with an Everclear song about an absent father. I never heard it on the radio, but I pulled it out from time to time. A form of forced suffering. A séance of sorts. I wanted to exorcise my demons. Stare them in the face.

I didn't want to keep going to bed with them.

I didn't want to keep falling in love with them.

But I would.

PUSH IT DOWN

"I KNOW it may sound surprising, from someone who fell into bed so easily with men she didn't care about. From someone who doesn't like to hug, or hold hands, but, my favorite thing to do is kiss. It's such an intimate thing, but I could kiss a beautiful man for hours. The next guy I would find myself caring about, god, he could kiss. But every time I think about the simple, somewhat innocent desire, I am pulled back to when it spiraled. Slowly, surely."

"Did he take something from you, this guy?"

It's still so fuzzy, so blurred. I can never name what it is, what it was. "He wanted to, and he wasn't the first, so I'm not surprised I push it down, away in the far corners of my mind. I explain it away, remember his lips on my own, how delicate he could be."

THE FRINGES

I'VE NEVER PAID much attention to other people's reputations. People like to talk, and everything said isn't always true. I know some pretty nasty shit has been said about me. Some may be true, most not. I'd been warned to stay away from Rich. People say he is bad news. And honestly, he looks like bad news. He has a mean face. It only seems warm when he smiles. He isn't my type. He wants me, so that doesn't work. What a laugh, right? I might as well tattoo daddy issues on my forehead. I want what I can't have. I didn't want Connor while I had him, not the way I do now. I've spent night after night obsessing over him. Sometimes I think I just need to go on a date with someone new. Make out with someone new. Drown myself in bad habits and cheap sweat. I think I may know exactly who to test that theory out on.

RICH WAS one of those guys you always saw on the fringes. I'd see him at a party with mutual friends. At the bar. Sometimes the guys would drag me to a Friday night football game at their old high school. Rich was always there. And he always flirted with me.

His voice was deep. He liked to call me "Mama". It drove me insane, but no one had ever called me that. It was ridiculous and annoying, but behind every eye roll was a smile. He told me every time he saw me that I would eventually go on a date with him. I always told him he didn't have a chance in hell. He, of course, was friends with Connor. I reminded him of this. His response didn't get much of an argument from me.

"Are you and Connor dating?"

"No," I said. I was sitting in the parking lot of the bar, with my car door open. Waiting for a drunk Blane to pay his tab.

"Then what does it matter?" His large hand was on my doorframe. His dark eyes were peering at me and I was avoiding them, avoiding the tingling of my flesh.

Rich had the most beautiful smile I had ever seen on a man. It lit up his face and lit up anyone he aimed it at. He had a mop of curly brown hair on his head and his eyes were like the sky on a moonless night.

"It matters because he's your friend, okay. It just matters." I hated being around drunk people when I was sober. I had no intention of going out that night. I was curled up in bed watching a Friends marathon when Blane texted me needing a ride. His booty call had stood him up.

"Well, if it doesn't matter to me and it doesn't matter to him, then I wouldn't sweat it."

"It doesn't matter to him?" I whipped my head, locking eyes with him. How did he know it didn't matter to Connor if he took me out?

"Well, no." Rich knelt down and leaned onto his heels. He had never been so close to me. I always danced away from him at the bar, at people's houses. I didn't want to feel the sliver of attraction I had to him. So I kept my distance. The scent of his cologne filled my tiny hatchback. He was sucking on a mint. "He's dating someone. Pretty sure."

I hated the way he said it. So casually. As if it wouldn't gut me. Why offer that reminder? I didn't know if Connor was still with Tracey, due to my social media blackout, but I assumed. Maybe Rich and Connor weren't close friends at all. I had never seen them together. I just knew of their friendship through the grapevine.

I looked at the clock in my car. 12:30 a.m. I was about to drive off and leave Blane behind. I didn't have time for this shit. I was wearing the shorts I often went to bed in, an old band t-shirt, and flip-flops. My long hair was in a haphazard bun. Rich drummed his fingers on the frame of my car, staring at my profile.

"So, are you in, Betty?" The first night he met me he called me Betty. When I asked him why, he said I reminded him of Betty Boop. Pale skin, dark hair, tits, and ass. I shoved him and avoided him the rest of the night. Now I kind of liked the nickname.

When he yelled it from across the bar, I turned my head. It was natural.

Movement in my rearview mirror caught my eye and I watched as Blane exited the bar. "Sure," I tossed the word out as I reached for my door. Rich stood and let me close it. He tapped on my window so I rolled it down. "Blane has my number." He was smiling. Victory finally in sight. The man in question opened my passenger door and dropped his tall form inside my tiny car.

"Hey, Blane buddy, your girl Gwen has finally agreed to let me take her out. You got my number still?"

"Yeah, man."

"Be sure that she gets it." He rapped his knuckles twice on the top of my car and walked into the night. When I turned to Blane, he was grinning ear to ear.

"What?" I spat.

"He's a moron."

"I know," I agreed, turning back, staring into the parking lot. "Give me his number."

28

FRAGILE, BREAKABLE

My first date with Rich was exactly the kind of date I liked to go on. It was at our bar. I was in a familiar setting. I felt safe. We sat at a table with all of Rich's friends. There was no one-on-one. No reason for me to feel nervous. I needed that. I needed this.

Rich behaved completely different that night, he was a stranger. His booming voice was low, subdued. When he spoke to me he leaned in close, so only I could hear him. The Rich I knew wanted to make sure everyone in the room heard his jokes, his stories. I didn't know this guy sitting next to me. Or maybe I did.

I had spent the weeks leading up to our date feeling him out through text messages. The Rich at the bar wasn't the Rich in private conversation. He didn't annoy the shit out of me, like I hoped. I would find myself smiling at my phone, getting a thrill when I saw his name there. I pushed our date off though. I made excuses, the way I always did. He called me out every time and I lied through my teeth. Redirecting the blame back to him.

When we finally set a date, he told me it was the last time he would ask or reschedule with me, so I stuck to it. I let him pick me up at my trailer. Rich never struck me as snobby, so I had no worries.

He opened my door and laughed when I struggled to pull myself up into his huge black pickup truck.

As the night went on I worried about my numb fingers, my smile that was on fire. The liquor mixed with his smile, it could be deadly. Our date was a midweek casual affair. I had to work the next day, so I told him I needed to be home by ten. When nine rolled around, I was regretting it. I wanted more time.

I looked over and saw his wrist resting on the table in front of him. He was turned away from me, talking to a friend, when I brushed my fingertips against his. The response was instant. He dropped his hand down and found mine. I knew I was in bad territory but I could not stop myself. Hand-holding on the first date? With a guy I always wrote off as a loud-mouth dick? It was the damn smile. The way his dark hair curled around his ears. He wasn't conventionally beautiful, or my type. He had a scruffy beard that didn't quite cover the acne scarring on his neck and jaw. He wasn't as tall as most of the guys I went after. When he smiled it made my stomach dip. It was different from the other times he had used it on me. He was enjoying himself with me. Enjoying the fact that I was having a good time, wondering if I was wrong about him.

When he dropped me off that night, I didn't ask him in. We sat in his truck and talked for a half hour past my self-imposed curfew. I couldn't stop chatting. I wanted to kiss him and I had to figure out how to initiate it. He was leaning back in his seat, angled toward me, but keeping his distance. All my instincts had told me he would be all over me if I went out with him. He was proving me wrong and it only made me want him more. I needed to taste him.

I told myself I had one more question and then it was time to woman up.

"So, you were pretty quiet tonight," I said, eyeing my porch light through the windshield.

"Yeah. I'm sorry about that."

"Don't be sorry. It felt like you were a completely different person. Which one is the real you?"

"Both," he laughed. "I just had a lot on my mind all night. I'm sorry if, for any moment, you felt like I wasn't having a good time. I've had the best time with you tonight. I almost canceled on you. I know you tried to cancel a million times though so I couldn't do it."

"Wait, why did you almost cancel?" I crossed my arms, but I wasn't pissed. I wanted to mock him, but the look on his face stopped me.

"I needed to get out of the house tonight. That's why I didn't cancel. My grandmother died this morning."

"Fuck, Rich. I'm so sorry. Seriously, you didn't have to go out with me tonight. I would have understood."

"I didn't want to though. It was a shitty ass day and I wanted at least one good thing to come from it. I've been wanting to see you and have this date for so long. And I'm glad I did. I had a great time tonight despite the shit in my head."

I leaned forward, untangled my arms, reached for his hand. I liked the way it fit into mine. It felt natural. Everything with him felt natural tonight. It was so unexpected, I wasn't sure where to go with it.

He looked at the clock on his dash and into my eyes. "You need to get inside, beautiful girl. You have to be at work early tomorrow."

"I know," I groaned. I attempted to pull my hand from his but he squeezed, pulling my gaze back to his.

"Thank you for taking my mind off of everything."

"No problem." My words were an awkward mumble. He had that look in his eye. I blushed and looked down at his lips. Full and pink. When he leaned forward, I came to him. The kiss was surprising. I felt it in my center. It kept going, and I felt my fingers curling into his shirt. When I pulled away, I didn't worry over embarrassment. "What the fuck?" I whispered.

"What?" he laughed, knowing.

"I didn't know you could kiss like that."

RICH and I didn't work out. The sex never thrilled me, never moved me the way his mouth did. I could kiss him for hours on end, but the chemistry stopped there.

"I'm going to be a disappointment," he said, as I straddled him on my rickety new bed. I shut him up with my lips, pulled his hair. "Just shut up and let me fuck you," I replied. I wanted to see if the drinks I had in my blood would make his dick as exciting as his mouth. It wasn't.

Jealousy was an issue too, control.

Our relationship evolved slowly into a beast with no name. We weren't lovers, but some nights he would come over and crawl into my bed. We would make-out, touch each other, I'd get him off if I was in the mood.

THEN, one night I picked him up from the bar and took him to his house. It was bare bones, a mattress on the floor. I look back on moments and wonder who can be trusted. I remember his weight on me, the press of my palms to his shoulders. He passed out eventually. My clothing was never removed, he never moved inside of me. *He didn't rape me; there was no damage done,* I thought.

I could feel it building up, this resentment inside of me, for everyone, every man.

I stopped taking his calls for a while, then felt guilty. His pleas were desperate, I was cold, and I convinced myself that my wild imagination was the enemy.

ONE NIGHT a mutual friend called me. He said Rich had been going on about me all night. They were both drunk and needed a ride home. So I hopped into my little hatchback and picked them up. Rich was all hands and poison. He told me I was a demon, that he couldn't stop thinking about me, that it wasn't his fault he could never be Connor. He told me he should have listened to his sister when she warned him away from me.

When I replied under my breath that his sister could kiss my ass, he lost his mind.

He told me that a cunt like me needed to keep his sister's name out of my mouth. That's when the wheels of my little car stopped moving, when my foot hit the brake.

I left him on the side of the road, took his friend home, and cried on the way back to my trailer.

It's such a silly thing, the way we let foolish boys fool us into thinking we are fragile, breakable, by their words. Our tears sometimes prove them right.

29

OH, THAT BITCH IS INSANE

HE SHOWED up at Paul's on a Wednesday. He showed up, wrecking everything, waking me up. I didn't think I would ever see Connor again. And there he was, walking in all casually, making me so nervous I wanted to throw my napkin down on the table and run to the bathroom to throw up. The guys told me his girlfriend cheated on him. I hated that that made me happy. I hated what kind of person that made me.

FOR AS LONG as I've been alive, people have told me that I'm not good at hiding my emotions on my face. I didn't like that about myself for years. I embrace it now, but back then I just wanted to hide away.

I was sitting at the table in the bar, staring down at my clenched fingers. It was the only way to make them stop shaking. They were gripped tight to my purse handle. My stomach was in knots and I felt like I was going into heat.

Connor sat there quietly talking to me like nothing was wrong, as if it was no big deal that we hadn't spoken in a long time.

It was just us at the table, our friends gone in search of their next round.

"So you're dating Rich, huh?"

"Sort of." I couldn't help the lie; he didn't need to know that was over, so fleeting. I wanted his jealousy, after months of silence. I stared at my drink in front of me, vodka and red and ice. I had barely touched it, the glass was sweating, though not nearly as much as I was.

"My *friend*, Rich." He lifted his glass to his lips, stared at the bar in the distance.

"Yes. Your friend. If it doesn't bother him, then it doesn't bother me." My words bit. I swallowed, heavy. I needed my drink, my fingers traced the cold glass, but I couldn't bring it to my lips.

"You've never let anything stop you from going for what you want, have you?" He looked at me then, his eyes black. I wanted to slap them shut, or see them roll back as I straddled him.

"No, I haven't. And that worked out well for you once. Didn't it?" I reached for my glass again, this time pulling it to my lips, letting my purse fall to the floor. My fingertips were wet, slippery. I tried to place the song that was playing in the background.

"I'm not so sure I'd call what we had 'working out well'."

I didn't know which way he was going. Playful or cutting? I could work with either one. "I'm sure you thought it was working out just fine when we went to that baseball game? When you fucked me at my place and then had a girlfriend the next Monday?" My jaw was set, my lips a thin line.

"I'm sorry about that." He sounded sincere, heavy and hurting. Not for me, for himself. I wanted to wound him.

"You're only sorry because she fucked you over. I'm glad she cheated on you." I wanted my words to be a slap, but he just nodded.

"She wouldn't be the first one."

"I never did." I hurt him. I knew that, but I was not what my parents were. A cheater. Not yet anyway.

"Because I never gave you the chance. You seem like the type." He shrugged his shoulder, such a casual insult, thrown from his wounding lips.

"I've never been unfaithful. Never in my life." It wasn't because I had never wanted to be. I'd wanted revenge from time to time. But that wasn't my style. My parents had done it and I never wanted to be like them in that way.

"Well, I've been cheated on by every girlfriend I've had."

I wanted to feel sorry for him but I was still stung by pumpkin-faced Tracey. By the winter I had spent alone. The baseball game. The way he dropped me. Maybe I deserved it, maybe not. "Maybe it's you then." I downed the last of my cranberry and vodka, avoided his eyes.

"Probably is." He lifted his own drink, downed it. "I like fucked up women. Project women. Maybe, just maybe, I have a savior complex."

"So good of you, Doctor, to self-diagnose yourself right here for me." I looked at the bar, my friends' backs were to us.

"Why shouldn't I? You were happy to do it for me."

I thought of the few texts I had sent Connor while he was with her. He had never responded. It should have turned me off but it made me want him more. His faithfulness, I wanted it. I hated myself for pissing it away, for taking him for granted.

"You want another drink?" He was pushing his seat back, looking me in the eye. He looked pretty smug for a guy who just had an ex tell him he was probably the reason his girlfriends cheated on him. It just showed me that he didn't give a shit about my opinions on his love life anymore. I was no longer a part of it.

"Yeah," I said, flippantly. I didn't want to lose my power.

As he walked away, Blane walked back over from the bar where he had been flirting with some chick I didn't recognize.

"Well, that didn't take long," he laughed, pulling a pack of cigarettes from his coat.

"It's not what you think." I punched him on the arm and looked over my shoulder, looking for Connor.

"It's not what it looks like? You're not still desperately in love with him? You're not looking at him like you want to crawl in his damn lap? He's not getting you another drink?"

"You're a real asshole, you know that?" I didn't really believe that. I liked that he called me on my shit.

"Yeah, that's why you adore me." Blane walked outside to smoke his cigarette so I pulled my phone from my purse. I had no messages waiting for me but I fiddled with it, hoping Connor would think I was texting Rich. Word traveled fast in our small group, so I kept my mouth shut about some things. No one knew I had left Rich on the side of the road last weekend. That we were done. I didn't think Rich even knew it yet. He was in denial. His texts, still traveling to my phone every day, proved that to be true.

I DIDN'T WANT it to, but it bugged me that Connor didn't have his shit together. Maybe it was because he had opportunities that I had never been given. I woke the next morning, to chaos.

His family wasn't filthy rich, but they had connections. Most people took advantage of those things. Connor rebelled against them. He had a classic car, so it never went out of style. His clothing was classic, so it never went out of style. He looked like a guy who had it together, but when I woke up in his new place the day after we met again at the bar, I knew he didn't.

I preferred him living in his sister's guest bedroom. At least then, things were tidy, quiet, respectable. I knew it felt like a prison to him then, and that was surely the reason for the trash heap I was opening my eyes to, but damn man.

The mattress was on the floor. His closet door was open, shoes, boxes, and jeans spilled out.

I liked the thought of him being single, living at his sister's house. I thought it would deter girls from wanting to be with him. Shallow girls, anyway. I wanted to be with him no matter where he was. But now, he was on his own. It would be easier to bring girls home. These were the things I thought about while we were apart. Reasons I hoped would be roadblocks, cock-blocks. The truth is if a guy wants to get laid, nothing is really going to stand in his way. But I needed comfort, anywhere I could find it.

Flashes of the night before flew around in my mind, swirling.

He was so drunk, we both were. He didn't want me, not really, but when a guy has enough shots he will take you home, think you're a good idea for long enough. Blane had thought I was stupid to get myself tangled up in Connor again, but he was the one who dropped us off at Connor's new place.

I could hear Connor's new roommates in the distance. I pulled the covers from my body and tiptoed around the room, searching for a bathroom. I knew there was one nearby. Connor had set me up on the countertop next to a sink, fucked me senseless, just a few hours ago. I stumbled to the door next to the closet, shuffled in, and sighed when I saw the toilet.

My eyes darted to the sink where my phone sat, vibrating and lighting up the room. I pulled up a text from Blane letting me know my car had been dropped off at Connor's. Maybe he knew I would want to be getting out soon.

When I crawled back into bed, Connor stirred but didn't wake. I heard his phone ding from the nightstand and my stomach somersaulted.

I wondered who was texting him. It would have been so easy to check, but I had never been that girl. I never snooped. I never stalked. I never wanted to know the bad things, the things that ripped my heart to shreds. I would gladly live in a land of denial.

I DIDN'T THINK I would see Connor again so soon. But later in the day, after I finished a TV dinner and settled down to watch The Shawshank Redemption for the third time that week, Blane called me. He had that tone in his voice, the one he got when he was excited about some new juicy gossip. He informed me that Connor's ex had found out we went home together. And she didn't take the news well. I couldn't believe my ears when he told me of the damage done. I had to see it for myself.

Connor's new vehicle, a Range Rover, was light colored, silver, gold, it depended on the light. The spot where Tracey, Connor's ex, carved my initials in with the fucking rock, were grey. You could see the frame of the car clearly. I had pissed plenty of people off in my life, but nothing to this extent. Nothing this crazy. He really drove girls crazy. I tried not to think of all he has made me think and feel. The mania he inspired in me. I had never been driven to this level.

I thought of the night he met me. Or the night he saw me. The broken glass. The blood, red, dripping on the carpet. I loved him in a way that was different than the way I loved Avery. That love was fading quickly, and would soon die completely. I didn't know it then, but summer would bring an interesting development. The year would bring more endings.

I WALKED up to Connor's new place and knocked on the door.

Connor answered in a towel. Surprised to see me. "Hey, what's up?"

I looked him up and down. It was less than twenty-four hours ago that he looked like this in his bathroom. Wet and clean after we showered the sex off our skin.

"I heard about your car. What the fuck?"

"Yeah," he replied, looking behind him to see if anyone else had heard in the house.

He stepped outside and his pale skin begged me to touch it. I could tell this wasn't something he wanted to talk about. And it was apparent that he hoped I wouldn't find out, but our small circle of friends loved to talk.

"Why didn't you tell me?"

"I didn't want you to think I was blaming you for it or something. Or to feel guilty in any way. She's crazy. It was your name, but it was me she was pissed at."

"Oh, that bitch is insane. Trust me, I wouldn't have blamed myself. I just wish you would have told me." I wanted him to tell me things, any god damn thing. But he was a steel trap. I had lucked out last night. He was offering me his skin again, but that heart of his was still long gone. Lost to me. I wondered then if I would ever get it back. I had no idea I would pummel it into the ground. I would later want to give anything to have the days when he loved me less back. When I was the one yearning. It was easier to manage. I could handle all of my sad wanting. It was his sadness that was too hard to bear.

30

CHOKE ON IT

"DID you ever forgive yourself for hurting him over Avery?"

"Yes. I was able to get over Avery that summer. We slept together again, and when he left, he told me I couldn't tell a soul that it happened. To choke on it. I wanted him to choke on it. To die inside a little, for me, for anyone."

"I'm glad you were able to see him for what he was to you."

"Me too. It occurred to me then how to get over someone. You can get over someone by getting back under them under the perfect circumstances. Avery cheated on his wife with me and that was the end of it all. The sick show was done, I was divorced from the want for him that had been so heavy in my veins for two years. For the two years we had been separate beings. I had built up this version of him that was more God than man. I convinced myself I had lost out on this faithful husband. When he fucked me I felt the dirty truth in my mouth, under my tongue. He was flawed, lesser. He was a dirty piece of shit. And okay, I was pretty pathetic, too. I had slept with a married man. I tried to justify it. This all-consuming love I had carried deep in my belly for him, I just wanted to be free of it. He just wanted to fuck someone that wasn't his wife and I was an easy target."

"Did you end up forgiving yourself for it?"

"Yes. But it took a little while. I hated my skin and the double-wide trailer I lived in. I was surprised he let his precious self in the door. Everything was crystal clear and it stung. I see everything now, I saw it then. He always made me feel small."

31

SILVER BAND

I DON'T KNOW what Avery's life was like anymore. He is married and he has a child, a stepdaughter. This whole life so separate from me. It's been two years since he was mine. His new family is Godly. I am nothing like that. I don't think of him much, but someone at work asked me about him. So I texted him on my lunch and he texted back. My hand shook as I typed his number into my phone. I wondered if he would have changed it but then I remembered he has had the same one since high school. I had never reached out to a married man before in my life. Women like that? I hated them. Now I knew their hearts. Now I was one of them.

AVERY LOOKED around my place and I shivered. He'd always placed such an importance on things. Where you lived, what you drove, what you wore. I got caught up in it all. And when he was gone, I started to value what was more important. Saving money. Just trying to survive on my own.

My home was my safe place. I very rarely let anyone inside. When I got together with a guy, I liked to go to his house. I didn't like having men in my bed. Now here was my ex, walking around, running his fingers along my belongings. On the things that made up my life after him. And I felt sick to my stomach. My bedroom door was open and he peered inside, then turned around, smiled at me, and walked in.

I shouldn't have followed him. I should have made him leave.

But I learned that night that he had a power over me still. And he was here. After two years apart.

I tried to ignore the silver band on his hand. I walked into my bedroom to find him standing at the side of my bed. He crawled into it like he lived there. Like he had always been there.

I walked over to my desk and pulled myself up onto it, crossed my legs, and stared at him. Beautiful Avery with the smile of a devil, of a snake.

"What are you doing over there?" he smirked.

I wanted to throw him out, or sit on his face. I wasn't sure which would be the better idea. I was starting to see what a mistake this was, starting to see him with the same eyes as everyone else, all the people who told me I was better off without him. "Wondering what you're doing," I said.

"Just making myself comfortable," he said.

I wanted to peel my skin off under his gaze. "I can see that," I said. There was no humor in my voice, in my eyes. The way his eyes held mine, it was obvious to both of us, he had the power here. I was trembling already and he hadn't even touched me. He was across the room, twisting me up.

I was disgusted with myself for wanting him still, but I did. I wanted to prove something to myself. This was how I won games. The ones others played and the ones I made up in my head.

"Come here," he said.

I shook my head, stared down at my dirty carpet.

"Come over here, now."

I didn't answer. I just got up and stood at the foot of the bed. I crawled across my comforter and propped myself onto one elbow, staring over him, into my open bathroom door. The trash was about to spill over the top.

"Look at me."

I hated his commands. I hated that they turned me on. I felt warm between my thighs. I shook my head again. In response, he pushed himself up and placed his palm on my shoulder, pressing me flat down.

I closed my eyes and felt a couple tears start to grow. I don't know if he saw them, if he cared.

He ran his nose along my jaw and I couldn't control the shaking anymore.

"You're so nervous," he said.

I knew he was laughing at me inside. This was just a game to him too, but I felt like I was going to break apart under his touch. The touch I longed for ever since he left. Part of me wanted to kick him out. The fact that he was here was enough. I had gotten what I wanted, for years. The proof that his marriage was unhappy. That his life after me was not perfect, wasn't the way it looked in pictures.

I moved to kiss him and he pulled away.

"Not yet." He continued to tease me, grazing his lips along my collarbone, pushing me down every time I tried to reach for him.

When he finally did kiss me, we didn't stop. He had pushed me too close to the edge.

I got on top of him and fucked him in a way that I never did while we were together. I showed him everything I learned from other men after he let me go. That I could control my pleasure and it wasn't just up to him. I made him look at me as he betrayed her. I wrapped my hand around his throat and watched his eyes as he liked it.

I thought being with him again would hurt me more. But instead, it woke me up. It showed me what kind of man he was. It showed me that if I got what I wanted, if I had gotten his last name all those years ago, that he would have betrayed me. He would've been fucking some other girl in her dirty trailer while I was taking care of a child.

I didn't come, and he didn't expect me to.

"You've never been able to get me there," I said, as he was pulling his jeans up, just an arm's length away. There. That was it. The punch to the gut. He looked me in the eye and hated me. I enjoyed it.

Before he left, he told me not to tell anyone what happened. He said he would burn my trailer to the ground if I did.

I washed my hands and took the makeup off my face as he gave me his speech.

I didn't care what he had to say.

Everything between us had lasted less than a half hour and in those thirty minutes, I stopped loving him.

Everything I held onto for all those years, every beautiful thing that I thought about him, fell away. I finally saw him for what he was. A shallow man who followed his dick around. A boy who loved toys only for a little while.

I had been one of them. I let myself be one of them again. But I had no interest in ever seeing him again.

I let him out of my bedroom, out of my living room, onto the front porch, out of my heart.

I shut the door behind him and didn't say a word.

When he pulled away, I fell to my knees and I cried. Not for him but for myself. What I let myself become. I slept with a married man. That was something I could never wash off. It didn't matter that he was mine first. He said vows to Wendy, and I let him break them with me.

I didn't tell any of my friends what I did, and I never heard from him again. When he was brought up in conversation it didn't hurt anymore. Whatever I saw a picture of him and Wendy online it didn't hurt anymore. Because I knew the lie that lived under the surface. I know the frailty of his love for her.

My own shame kept me quiet. I had become the kind of woman that I swore I never would. I thought of the little boy, Avery's little boy. And I hated myself.

The only good that came from that night is that I stopped loving him there instantly. But a little bit more of the little amount of love I had for myself fell away, too.

32

UNRESTRAINED

"So you never saw your ex again? Avery? That was it?"

"Yes. Finally. I was free and it felt good. I spent the rest of the summer sleeping with Connor, with Joe, hanging out with the guys. I was drinking until I blacked out, waking up with bruises, teetering on the edge. I was fighting with my mother about talking to my stepfather, feeling guilt over a beast in my stomach that I had no name for. It wasn't time for me to wake up and I wasn't sure I wanted to."

"When would you?"

"It was 2009 then, but in 2012 the fog would be lifted. I would take my skin off and become a new person, some mute shell, a closed door. Connor would be there when I figured it all out. He was always there, it seemed. Even when he wasn't."

"And he didn't want to get back together?"

"No. He wanted to fuck and have fun and slip in and out of each other's bedrooms. I did that with him for so long. I let myself be the *fun fuck* and the *almost-girlfriend*. I let him be that until our games put me in the hospital."

"How did you end up there?" Her eyes go wide.

I always forget to be careful with my words. It sounds like he beat me, but that was never him. His dick, the cause of all this bullshit, put me there. "We were having sex one night and afterward I felt funny. I slept on his bathroom floor the whole night, sweating, feeling like I was dying. I told him to go to work the next day. Not to worry about me, but he should have. I couldn't walk, so I had a friend come get me from his house to take me to the hospital. I passed out at the front desk of the emergency room while trying to fill out my paperwork. A cyst had burst inside of me the size of a baseball. The blood was swirling, unrestrained, in my body. I had to have a transfusion, surgery."

"Oh wow. Did Connor come see you?"

"No. He didn't. I stopped loving another man that year. I stopped and I pushed him away, for as long as I could."

33

"DO THAT AGAIN."

I FEEL like I can finally move again, be normal. The past few months have been rough. I've been going to work, taking it easy, then coming home. It's a nice routine. TV dinner, wine, 9 p.m. bedtime. I don't text Connor back. He kept texting for a while. I don't know how someone can be so thick, so damn stupid. How can he think we can go back to normal? He didn't visit me in the hospital after what happened. I spent days alone in my trailer. He went out of town that weekend. Doing who knows what. Seeing who knows who. I have no desire to see him again. There will be no more fucking. No more late-night meetings. Thanksgiving is next week and I think I may actually be up for going out on Wednesday. Everyone is out the night before Thanksgiving. I can't sit at home while all my friends are out on such a busy night. Maybe I'll see Connor and be able to blow him off. I want to do it in person. I want to snub him. He deserves it. And I deserve some of my pride back.

THE GUYS PICKED me up at seven. We were going to a new bar in town. I was happy about that. Going to a fresh place on my first night out in a while felt perfect.

When we made it inside, the boys scattered. I found an empty barstool at the end of the bar.

It didn't bother me that the guys left me alone. The car ride was filled with questioning. *How are you? What happened? Where have you been?* I eventually told them I loved them but they needed to lay off until I got a drink in me.

The new bar was a sports-themed bar. TV screens lined the walls. The waitresses were dressed up in skimpy referee outfits. I pulled my phone up and hid my face, hid my survey of the room.

I saw Rich in a far corner talking to some friends. I made a mental note to avoid that part of the bar. When the bartender came over, I ordered a cape-codder and swiveled my stool. My spot at the bar ended at the wall. No one could sneak up on me if I turned just the right way. I wasn't in the mood for an ambush, for drama.

From across the room, I recognized the younger brother of a guy who always hit on me when I saw him at the bars. His brother was a no-go but the younger one was a different story. They didn't look related at all. The older brother had dark hair. He was thin, squirrelly, and you could tell every word that fell from his lips was a lie.

I had never spoken to the younger brother. He was a couple years my junior and beautiful. He was also built. I knew he had been in the army for a few years. I wondered if he was still in and just home for the holiday, or if he was out now. He was chatting with a few guys I recognized.

I let my eyes flitter his way a few times throughout the night. Mostly I stayed to myself. My decision to go out hadn't been the best one. I was still nursing my wounds. Tending to my broken wing. Luckily, Connor didn't show up.

At 11:30, the guy who had been sitting next to me finally left. Or, was dragged out. He looked to be in his 60s or so and was drinking alone the whole night. A younger man, possibly his son, came to pull him out. I felt a slow hand reach over my heart, give it a tug. I would be alone tomorrow for the holiday. I was no better. I shouldn't feel sorry for him, some of us chose that, to be alone when the calendar told us we should be with others.

I buried myself in my phone after he left, cringing at the thought of Rich finding his way to the empty chair.

When someone reached for it, I was startled by the sight of the hand. It was the younger brother I was eyeing earlier. He smiled at me when I looked at him. He had nice teeth, nice lips. Amber hair glittered on his jaw in the low bar light.

"Hi." His eyes were blue, his hair short. He had a nice voice. There was no heavy bass to it, which warmed me.

"Hey." I sounded shy, *I was shy*. I looked back into my phone. I had enough alcohol in me. I knew I could charm him, but it felt useless. The truth was I just wanted Connor. I wanted him to be the way he was last year so I could love him again. The nice guy, the one who cared about me. He screwed it up, I screwed it up. It was so exhausting.

My new barstool neighbor interrupted my thoughts.

"I'm Chadwick," he said.

"I know," I replied, smiling at his formal name. Why not just go by Chad? "Your brother hits on me all the time." I wrapped my lips around my straw.

"Well, he's a jackass and I'm the better brother." He chuckled to himself.

I liked the way his shoulders shook. They looked solid. I imagined him throwing me over one, carrying me out. I hadn't had a sexual thought in a while. When sex lands you in the hospital, you tend to avoid even the casual daydream. "That much is apparent." I laughed.

"Has my brother ever asked you out?" He glanced around the bar, finding his sibling; I followed his gaze.

"Yeah."

"What do you say when he does?" He was turned back to me, swiveled in his stool a bit, his knee inches from mine. I wanted to shift and push out that extra space.

"I say no and remind him he's married." I turned a little, let my leg touch his.

"God, he is such a dumbass." He shook his head, his eyes closing a little.

I liked his eyelashes, the wrinkle of his eyes. He seemed soft and I needed soft. "Are you going to ask me out then? Is that what this is?" I ran my thumb along my bottom lip, pretended I wanted to hide my smile.

"I don't know, are you going to turn me down?"

I should have said no. I was half a woman, half an open wound, and I was scared to have sex. After what happened with Connor.

"I'd say yes." I turned forward, pulling my knee from his.

"Then yes. I'm asking you out." He tapped the bar, pulling my eyes to his hands. He was good at this. I wanted them on me then.

In response, I grabbed his phone from the bar, put my number in it. "Okay. Let's do it then."

I paid my tab and found the guys, not wanting to linger, to leave on a good note.

I LEARNED that Chadwick lived on the other side of the city. It took me a good hour to make it to his house for our first date. I didn't want him coming to my place. He drove a little green Audi and didn't work. The army was paying him to go to school full-time to be an engineer. Blue collar men made me feel at ease. Chad's ambitions made me feel small, but also excited. His skin begged me to touch it and we went on our first date knowing I would be staying the night. We both drank. I wasn't driving my car while under the influence and I wouldn't ask him to call me a cab. He took me to a sports bar and I drank my nerves away. From there we went downtown.

When he reached for my hand, I didn't pull away. Holding hands was such an intimate act for me. I always avoided it.

CHAD'S HOUSE was nicer than I expected. Too nice for a guy who wasn't even working. The only way he was swinging it was because he was renting a room from a friend.

His bedroom made me pause as soon as I saw it. It looked like an adult's bedroom. Every guy I met had a bedroom that looked like a frat room, a kid's room. Shit on the floor, a comforter that didn't match the sheets, clutter.

He had a large black four post bed. On top of it was a large white down comforter. I walked into his room and took in the rest; a desk, a bookcase full of books. Everything was clean and tidy. Sure, he could have been a mess and only cleaned because he knew I was coming over, but sometimes a little bit of effort was nice when most dudes put in none. I pulled myself onto the bed, nervous. The kissing downstairs had been heated, desperate. The walk up the stairs had given me time to wonder what I was doing, if I would sleep with him, maybe fool around a little, or just pretend I was tired and go to sleep.

Chad walked in and closed the door. He looked shy. "Ready for bed?" he asked.

"Sure." I blushed.

He pulled his shirt over his head in front of me and answered my question. Yes. I would be sleeping with him.

I had never seen a man built like him. Perfect lines, tan skin. He reached for the button of his jeans and slid the zipper down. His pecs moved like slow water.

"Stop," I said, stilling him.

"What?" he asked, his voice a whisper, alarmed.

"Do that again." The words felt like smoke, falling from my lips.

Watching him undress was art. I wanted to savor it, for him to rewind and repeat. I could get over Connor with this guy, I felt it, the slow ache of my heart, easing. The dull pain floating away. If it didn't work, maybe there would be some nice sex to come from this. I liked Chad's side of town. None of my friends were here. No one knew me here. I could pretend I wasn't the trailer park slut, the trashy girl who blew it with the decent guys. I could blow it with this decent guy and no one would know.

No tally mark on my coffin.

WHEN WE WOKE the next morning, he was spooning me. The sun snuck through his white curtains. Everything looked new in his room. A piece of black and white art hung above his dresser, a train in motion. This guy was different. I could feel it, but I didn't trust my feelings. Why should I?

When Chad smiled at me after waking up, I felt a pang of guilt. It didn't feel like a one-night stand. I could see myself making more and more trips. Maybe it would become a Wednesday night ritual.

He told me to call him when I got home so he knew I was safe.

I did and we talked for an hour. He asked me to come over a few days later, the night before I had a day off again.

It was such a strange thing. I had been single, broken up from Avery, for over two years, and this was the first guy to have me come stay at his place. Was that right?

I ran through the men I had been with.

There was Daniel, so soon after Avery, before Connor, who wanted me to come over. But I had fled after that one-night stand. He had been so tender, said he wanted to put me back together. The alcohol had landed me in his arms and he had that look in his eyes. The kind that said he wanted to find a wife. I wasn't ready for that kind of thing.

Blane, yeah, I had stayed at his house, but only after a party when I couldn't drive.

When we were dating, Connor didn't invite me over because he lived with his sister so we always stayed at my place.

Rich lived with his parents, too. Damn. I really needed to date more men who had their shit together. Not that me living in my uncle's trailer was much better, but still.

I needed someone with his shit together so I could get mine together. We couldn't be two losers in love.

There is a certain hope that tattoos your soul when you meet someone new. Someone promising. I felt it then. But as always, it would be short lived.

HIS MERCY

I WANTED to tell Chad that the hockey game was a bad idea, but I didn't. What could I say? He had the tickets already. I just focused on the hockey players on the ice. I tried to forget that I had been down on that ice. That Connor had held my hand, my elbow, kissed my hair. I pretended this date was better than that date, even though it couldn't be.

I GOT the jumbo popcorn and a drink. I held Chad's hand in the bitter cold of the rink. The air stung but I smiled. After the first period, I pulled my phone out and took a selfie with Chad. I uploaded it to my Instagram while he got us more refreshments. I wanted everything to appear picture perfect, even if it didn't feel that way.

The text came sooner than I thought it would. Connor's name lit up my phone and I felt a strange mixture of anger and gratification. I knew he would see it, but I couldn't keep my social media hidden, pretend I wasn't dating someone new.

Connor: I know that guy. Chad, right?
Me: Yes.
Connor: He's a good guy.

I shoved my phone back into my purse. What was that? He was a good guy? Yeah, I was aware. It felt like a dig. Or it felt like a blessing. I didn't want a blessing. I wanted him to hate anyone I was with. I wanted him to want to trade places with whoever I was with. I pulled my phone back out and pulled up Facebook. Connor had been checked into the blue stadium an hour earlier.

No, wait, he hadn't checked in; he had been checked in by some chick. I clicked on the profile and took in the girl's blonde hair. No wonder he had been leaving me alone. He was seeing someone new. But still, he felt the need to reach out to me. Why? I searched the crowd. Did he know where I was sitting? He wouldn't be down here with us. He would be up in a shiny room with glass windows. With his date and sister and her husband. Bringing a girl here had to mean something, right?

Like it meant something with me? I wondered if they had skated in the dark like he and I had. In her picture, she looked tall, graceful. She probably knew how to ice skate. They probably held hands, glided across the ice like angels or some shit like that. No, Connor was no angel.

I heard a voice to my right. "Don't," Lesley said.

"What?" I blanched. I knew she knew. Those damn emotions and my damn traitor face.

"Stop looking for him. You're here with Chad. Chad is good for you." My friendship with Lesley was on solid ground, at the moment. She had no clue I had slept with Avery. If she knew, she would be done with me. I no longer was stung by her friendship with Wendy. Maybe I was growing up, or something like it.

"Well, maybe I'm not good for him." I didn't know if I believed it or not. We had been having fun. He was so nice, no drama, and here I was, looking for some guy I hadn't really dated in two years.

"Are you kidding?"

"I'm good for no one." How could she argue? In the past, she sabotaged half of my relationships. No, I sabotaged them, she ridiculed them. She liked Chad though. Hell, she probably wanted to fuck him. No, that was just me being cruel. She never gave off those vibes. Not with him.

Did Connor know it was my birthday? He was ruining it. Taking my happy from me. He couldn't have known I would be here. I didn't choose this place. I wasn't asking for this trouble.

CHAD TOOK me home that night. I let him into my trailer and into my bed. It didn't matter how many times we fucked, letting him into my home, it was more intimate. I had seen his shiny car, his tidy room. Now he could see my mess. Maybe he would stay around for it. Who knows. I wanted him to.

Just before Chad fell asleep, he spoke into my hair from behind. "I really like you, Gwen." It was a small thing but it made my heart hurt, because at that very moment, I was thinking of Connor, of ways to end this almost-relationship so I could be free to go to his house, to be at his mercy.

I was weak and looked at Connor's Facebook the next day after Chad left. He wore that fake smile, the one he always used in photos.

He could never smile for real. He reminded me of the episode of friends where Chandler couldn't smile for the camera.

In my sadness, I told myself he was using a fake smile because he didn't like the girl he was with.

I always hid from the truth.

35

VARIETY PACK

"How long did you date Chad?"

I think back, count on my fingers. "A few months maybe."

"What happened?"

"He was such a nice guy. I loved staying with him. I loved sleeping with him. He took me on dates, told his friends about me. It was what I wanted, but it wasn't with who I wanted it with. The shadow of Connor was still there. Eventually, I started answering Connor's texts, but I would not meet him. I would not see him. When he found out about Chad, he respected it. At first."

"How did he stop respecting it?"

"I didn't hear from Connor for three more weeks after the hockey game. I was having Valentine's Day dinner with Chad. My phone lit up and Connor asked me if I was busy. I knew what that meant. He wanted to fuck. I told him I was having Valentine's dinner with Chad and hid my phone. He responded that I should come over after I was done. The old me would have run over. Or lied. Said I was just in a movie with a friend. I always wanted him to think I was on the edge of my seat, waiting for him to ask me to come back to him, for real. But I was tired of that. I was tired of the way that made me feel. And then I learned from the guys he was seeing two girls. Not just the blonde, but a redhead, too. I would joke back with him, and say 'You're really trying to hit the whole variety pack, aren't you? A redhead a blonde, and you want to add me, the brunette, back in, huh? Not happening.' He would laugh it off, still pursue me. It was always this thing with us before we got together. Constant chasing and other people and never being happy with the stand-ins but pushing each other away when we were free to be together. I was just so tired of it."

"Why did things end with Chad?"

"It was embarrassing, really. He asked me to be his girlfriend and I said yes. Then the nice guy turned into an ass and wouldn't even accept my relationship status on Facebook. That's a silly thing, right?"

"A relationship is still a relationship without social media validating it, but it was important to you, right?" She always makes me answer my own questions, turns it back to me and my wants, what I think it's supposed to mean.

"Yes."

"Then it wasn't a silly thing." She taps her fingers on the bar. "Did you run back to Connor?"

"No. He was hanging out with the redhead still. The blonde was long gone. I let him come to me. Let him back into my bed, until I couldn't. He made me hate myself. He made me hate who I had become. Nothing was ever going to work out with anyone, as long as he was around. So one night I said I was done. I stopped answering his texts, and that lasted two weeks."

36

THE HEART IS A BEAST

I DIDN'T *like running away from places I found comfort in. I would often stand my ground, but gentle escapes were allowable. I didn't go by the old watering hole often, but I was not hiding from it. I just needed a new place. A place where Connor and any other ex wouldn't show up. When Joe called me up to tell me he was in town, I jumped at the opportunity to hang out with him. I hadn't seen him since the first night I hung out with Connor. He was the guy I left with.*

JOE WAS SOFT-VOICED AND DELICATE, the most enthusiastic lover I had ever had. He was the second person I ever slept with, right after dumping my first boyfriend of four years, when I was twenty-two. We never dated, but our friendship was easy, and five years later, we still had fun in bed.

He was the one I ran to after Avery dumped me. He was easy to run to because it never meant anything. It was blind touching, simple desire, easy to wash off. No guy I had ever been romantically linked to liked Joe. He was quiet, an observer, wealthy. He pulled jealousy from them easily. It was fun to hurt those who had hurt me with his want for me.

For Joe, I was once a cheap thrill. We fucked in cars, in his lake condo, wherever we could. We said goodbye with no words. I needed a nothing relationship like that sometimes. To cleanse the palette.

Joe ordered my drinks when we were out. I didn't mind. He paid too, so how could I argue? It was a Thursday night when everything changed. When I would have to give all the tricks, all the games, up for good.

Vodka made me pliable, loose, and sometimes fire, angry and coiled tight, ready to strike. I had downed three that night. Joe's hand was on my leg under the table. It felt warm there, my eyes wrinkled with laughter. Joe's friends did not run in my circle. I liked that about him, too. I had known him since I was fifteen, twelve years. He had an endless list of acquaintances. There was never a worry of anyone wondering who I was. I liked the anonymity.

Joe didn't show affection in public. I remember a time when I put my hand on his leg at the bar and he pulled it away. He screamed my name when we were alone, so vocal, so obedient. But in public, we were not to touch. I was a dirty secret, the dirty poor girl.

My phone buzzed on the table just as I was reaching for Joe's hand beneath the table. I pulled it up onto the table, flipped it over. My stomach fell, heat flushed my cheeks.

Connor's name lit up my screen. He was calling, not texting. That never happened, but I guess ignoring him had pulled it out of him.

"Excuse me," I said, dropping down from my chair, walking to the ladies' restroom.

"Hello," I hissed into my phone, pushing the swinging door in front of me open.

"Gwen?"

"Yes. What's up?" Why are you calling me? *Why why why?*

"Where are you?"

"What?" It was a lame reply, but why was he wondering where I was? We weren't together. He had seen to that. He didn't deserve to know where I was; I didn't owe him an answer.

"Where are you?"

"Why?" My voice was flat as I leaned against the tile of the women's restroom wall.

"Tell me where you are please. I want to come get you."

"Come get me for what?"

"You know."

Really? He was on this again? I wanted more. An *I'm ready to be with you.* "Yeah. I do. I don't need you for that. I'm busy tonight."

"Busy with who? Rich?"

"No." My voice was firm. No room for questioning. I didn't want to see Rich again, why was he so hung up on that one? I didn't want to see any of them again. All of the men who had ripped me open. Joe was safe and easy. There was no chance I would fall for him. I was beneath him. He was just biding his time until he found a Barbie girl. And that's what he would eventually marry.

THAT NIGHT I slept on Joe's houseboat. When I woke up, my phone showed me several missed calls from Connor. It was unlike him to appear so desperate. My phone died before I could make a decision on how to respond.

I drove home in a haze, muddled. I wanted to get home to charge my cell. I wanted to keep it off for days. I couldn't keep up anymore. With the back and forth. The sex and the way I choked on my feelings. I never brought up the fact that I still loved him. I just wanted to be with him, any way that I could. But it was draining me, draining my affections for him. How many years could I carry on being nothing more than a fuck buddy to a man who adored me once? I didn't mean to fall in love with him when it was already too late. I didn't mean to be a mess when he met me.

When I got home, I didn't have to make the decision on when to talk to Connor. He was standing on my porch. I pulled in, next to his Range Rover, and turned my engine off. We locked eyes through the glass, and I wanted to cry a little. Instead, I stared at my hands that found their way back to the top of my steering wheel. My knuckles were white and my stomach was a mess.

There are things you can't explain in life. Connor was one of them. My feelings for him, I couldn't paint a picture for anyone that would do my heart justice. I tried to love other men. I tried to move on. I convinced myself I did, a few times. My friends hated him at times. Hated me at times for my foolish desire to pin him down. The heart is a beast. A feral monster. And mine wanted this heart. Mine wanted Connor and no one else. And even as I knew that, I was always wondering why I was letting myself break all my rules.

It's a sad thing to desire being right more than you desire love that will not die. If this was it. If this was him wanting to be with me, would my heart change? Would my love fall away once it was returned?

YET TO COME

"I KNEW it wasn't going to be easy to give up my freedom. I had been single for three years. I rocked back and forth on what I wanted. I wanted to take a shower with someone every night. I wanted someone to travel with. I wanted to stay out late with my friends and never have to text anyone. To never have to tell anyone where I was. There was still a thrill in the thought of having a one-night stand. The feeling of someone's hands on me. Someone I barely knew and would never have to see again. I liked that kind of power. And maybe, deep down, I liked what Connor and I had. The sex was great, thrilling, and we would lose that when we both eventually loved each other at the same time. I don't know. I sometimes wonder if I even knew the girl I was back then."

"But he was ready, right? To be with you when he showed up on your porch?"

"I think he thought he was."

"And you?"

"I was in it more than him." I laugh. "But the worst was yet to come."

LOVE ME LESS

I WALKED up to my steps, fumbling with my keys, past Connor. He watched me open my door and stood outside as I walked past my couch. When I didn't hear him behind me I turned. "Come in."

"I didn't want to assume."

"Whatever." I waved my fingers in the air and threw my purse on my recliner. It was more of a catch-all than anything else. I didn't have much furniture, just leftovers that didn't belong to me.

I walked to the fridge for a bottle of water, my ears perked, mapping Connor's movements in my trailer. He was walking into the kitchen too, so I grabbed another bottle. I tossed it to him, wondered if the tension in the air slowed it down. I could still feel Joe's body on mine, his scent.

"Why are you here?" I asked after swallowing a mouthful of water.

"I wanted to see you."

"It's a little early in the day for you to want to see me. It's normally after nine, at the earliest, that you find your way into my life." I waited for him to ask me where I was the night before. I knew it was bubbling under the surface. I wanted him to ask, so I could tell him it wasn't any of his business.

He never asked. Instead, he stunned me.

"I think we should be together." He set his water bottle on the table next to him, crossed his arms.

It wasn't romantic, it felt like he was closing a deal. My heart thundered in my ears.

"We're together right now." I gestured between us with my arm. This wasn't how I expected this to go down. Mostly I convinced myself the day would never arrive, but on the few days or few moments I let myself believe Connor would one day want to be exclusive with me, it wasn't like this. It was softer, less like an aggressive job interview.

"You know what I mean." He scrunched up his face, creating ugly lines.

"No." I put the cap back on my water bottle. "I guess I don't know what you mean." I wanted him to do better. To say something nice. I knew I would say yes, I knew I would be his, as sad as that sounded, but I needed more.

"I think we should be a couple."

"What's wrong with what we've been doing?"

"You want to keep doing that?"

"No, and we both know that. But I want to know why you want this."

"I don't want you to be with anyone else but me. I don't want to keep seeing you just at night."

"That's been your choice. Not mine. I tried. For years. I've been hanging on to you for years. You know that, right?"

"Yes."

"Last September, we were sleeping together. And Blane told me he texted you and told you happy birthday. Do you remember what your response was?"

"No."

"You said 'Thanks, but I wish I had someone to spend it with'." I was going to cry, I could feel it bubbling up. My throat was on fire. "I wanted to be with you. I was in love with you, and you knew it. And you wanted him to feel sorry for you. Like you were alone. Like you didn't have me desperately wanting you, waiting for you."

"I know. I'm sorry." His hands were on his hips, he stared at the ceiling.

"And then I end up in the hospital. Because of you. Because finally having sex with you hit me even harder. I wasn't just broken emotionally, but physically. And I had to beg you to come see me." The tears started to fall. My grip on the water bottle threatened to pop it.

"I know. And I'm so sorry for that, too. I just hate hospitals."

"I don't give a shit!" It was all tumbling out, the hate and the hurt, the clotting. "I do too, but I was in one, because of you. I couldn't let anyone touch me for what felt like forever after that. And it wasn't just because I was afraid that something like that would happen again, which yeah, that was a fear. But it was because I couldn't stand to let myself care for anyone again. You fucked me up and I wish I could go back to the days when I hurt you. When it was just you, and not me."

"Then do it. Love me less. Let me pass you. Let's try. Let me fall again and let it hurt me more. But just try."

"I hate you. I wanted this for so long. I bit my tongue and killed myself inside, just so I wouldn't inconvenience you. So I could be the convenient fuck you would turn to. I just wanted you to spend time with me, and change your mind about me."

"It worked."

I wanted to fight with him more. I wanted to put up more of a fight. But I didn't. I drank the rest of my water and I tossed the bottle at him. Then I walked to him and let him pull me in.

When I pulled away, I walked to my shower, to wash off the scent of another man from my flesh, so I could start my new relationship with the one I actually wanted.

PART III

AUGUST WAS IN MY HEART

"WHAT WAS IT LIKE? Finally being together?"

"I wrote it on the calendar, our anniversary. And we would celebrate that date in May for years, until I left him. But he wasn't committed to me. I think he wanted to be. I think he feared I was on the edge of walking away. Maybe the thing with Chad pushed him to it. I had dated a nice guy and he figured, eventually, I would find one that would make me forget him."

"What do you mean when you say he wasn't committed?"

"I'm certain, that for a little while, he was seeing other girls. Hanging out with them. I was still timid, still trying to be what I thought he wanted. Some nights, he wouldn't want to hang out. And I think he had someone over. I never said anything. I choked on it, again. I just handled it the only way I knew how to."

"How's that?"

"An eye for an eye. Joe finally found his way back to the family business. The business I was working at. We were working together, one-on-one, due to a promotion at work. We would travel out of state together. So I let myself fall back into his arms. No one was looking, Connor wasn't jealous then. And I think it's because he knew he was guilty, too."

"That seems like a really sad way to enter into a relationship."

"It is. That's why I never told anyone what I felt I knew he was doing, and I never want that confirmation. I never let anyone know what I was doing. I wanted us to eventually even out, to stop lying to each other."

"And did you?"

"It took a few months, but yes. One day he told me he loved me and he was different. He was the guy from two and a half years before. The one who adored me and worshipped me. He never left my trailer. He cooked for me. He made love to me and he told me he loved me every morning and every night. He would text me in the middle of the day. So in my heart I told myself that even though May was on the calendar, August was in my heart."

40

YOU TRIED

It's been so long since I've shared a space with someone. Three years since I moved out of the house I shared with Avery. My trailer is too small for Connor and me, but we want to be together all the time. It's like a switch has been flipped. He's different. I wanted to tell him I loved him right away. I was in love with him for two years but I was sitting on the words. And there's this other part of me, the one that wants a guy to say it first for once, that is winning. I am tired of loving more. I've thrown my mother's advice out the window and it's always ended badly. I'm glad I waited. I'm glad I let him say it first. I think he loved me back then. When we were on that dance floor in the bar, years ago, before I ruined it all, I saw it in his eyes. And it can't compare to the way it felt to hear it from his lips.

I WAS NOT A GOOD COOK. I never learned. My mother worked hard when I was an adolescent. She still works hard. When she got off work, the last thing she wanted to do was cook for her kids. Now that I am adult, working hard at my job, coming home worn to the bone, I get it. I don't want to slave over a stove either. And I saw this praise for the women who did. I heard what wonderful, beautiful women they were because even though they were tired, they cooked a meal for their family. It wouldn't be the first time I lined myself up to an invisible measuring stick. It wouldn't be the first time I measured my worth as a woman upon dated ideals.

Anxiety was a foreign word then. I didn't know why I found it so hard to focus, why I rushed through things. Why the directions of a recipe made me anxious and sweaty.

I just wanted to eat a bowl of cereal for dinner. To heat up leftover pizza for breakfast. There were things I missed from the years I spent alone. I mourned them, but it was worth it to be with Connor. I reminded myself of that as I stared down at the hot grease in the frying pan on my stove.

One of Connor's favorite foods was fried chicken. I told myself I would make it for him for his birthday dinner, despite the gnawing in my belly. I would rather bake something, set a timer, let something marinate. Anything but this. I looked at the directions twenty times as I lay in bed after work. I knew I was going to fuck it up. I always did when I was trying to make something on the stove. If the day ever came when my eggs over easy didn't have to be turned into scrambled because I fucked them up, I'd probably keel over and die.

I stared at the chicken thighs on the countertop, determined to pick one. I couldn't stand over the hot grease forever.

When the hot oil hit my forearm, I let out an unearthly cry, inhuman. My skin went pale white, then red. I ran for my phone on the dining room table, the linoleum slick beneath my feet. More grease had fallen there.

"Hello?" Connor's voice on the other end of the phone was a salve for most hurts these days, but not for the current one.

"Hey," I grimaced, "I burned myself making the chicken. Can you pick up some bandages?"

"Are you okay?" I heard the music in his Range Rover muffle, the sound of his blinker.

I looked down at my arm. The skin was bubbled up. How many degrees was that? How bad would the scarring be? "No." My voice broke. The numbness of my arm ricocheted into a blinding pain skittering over a dull ache.

"Okay, I'll be there as soon as I can." My forearm would forever wear a scar the size of my palm. Connor cleaned and bandaged me up. I apologized and cried. I only wanted to give him a gift for his birthday, one that couldn't be bought with money, since I didn't have much.

Connor finished his own birthday dinner but I didn't have much of an appetite, and I didn't like fried chicken much anyway. I made it for him.

"I don't care about the dinner," he said in bed later, running his fingers over my collarbone. "I appreciate the thought, that you tried. That's what I love about you."

Years later, when I turned to stone and apathy, he would bring that night up. He would refer to it as one of the nights I still loved him. When I still tried, when I wanted to impress him.

THOSE FIRST TWO years were a blur. Connor moved out of the house he shared with his friends and back in with his sister in Lafayette Square, but it was as if he moved in with me, and his room there was just a storage space. My trailer was too small for him to fit all of his belongings in anyway.

I still worked at my same, draining job. I worked hard and found myself at the end of promotion after promotion. Connor would be proud one minute, taciturn the next. He didn't like me working for Joe's family, and with Joe. He didn't like me going on trips with Joe. But that relationship was now strictly professional. We weren't even friends and never had been. When the sex faded away, we were left with nothing.

Connor loved bringing home potted plants for me. I collected them, watered them, let them die. I was never good at nurturing. The only time in my life I had a knack for it was in those beginning years. I nurtured Connor, and he nurtured back. I still miss those moments.

41

BROKEN GLASS

Connor

"I BOUGHT A HOUSE TODAY, TWO ACTUALLY," I said it casually. Like it was no big deal. But it was, and I was excited. I probably should have told her, but it just sort of happened. I was having lunch with a friend when an old college buddy of his walked into the restaurant. He was a realtor and he joined us. We started talking about our jobs and these great listings he had. The next thing I knew, I was meeting him after work, looking at places. Gwen had been sick and I wasn't seeing her that night.

When I signed the papers on the house, I didn't wonder if she would get pissed that she hadn't been a part of the process. I didn't even know if I wanted her to move in.

We had been together for two years, and I was practically living in her trailer. I spent at least five nights a week there. The other two I was at my sister's house. I needed a place of my own.

I could see her excitement mixed with her fear. We often went to bed with words lodged in our throats. Part of me wondered if I was only telling her because she would find out eventually.

Some days, when she wasn't working, she never left her bed. She hated doing the dishes, that task often fell on me. I reminded her that her scuffed linoleum needed mopping.

On the few nights I stayed at my sister's place, I felt a calm rush over me. My sister stayed home with her children, her house was pristine. She even cleaned my bathroom. Gwen kept her trailer tidy, for the most part, but the deep cleaning was neglected. It was done after my urging, after I helped. It wasn't even my place. I would never live in a trailer. Not for real, anyway.

I almost left in the beginning, a year in. I couldn't figure out her mood swings. The way her brow would furrow. The way she could spit fire. I was ready to leave and then her car broke down. I always had a deep compulsion to take care of her. No one else was. She wasn't even taking care of herself. I felt like I needed to be the one to do it.

I felt like I needed to make sure she never became broken glass again.

42

THIN ICE

I WANT to write something here that I will remember fondly for many years to come. But I can't. Connor bought two houses without telling me. He said it was a spur of the moment thing, he went to look at a house and it was a great deal so he bought it. Then the realtor found another great deal, so he bought that one, too. Here I am, not sure I will have enough money to buy him a birthday present, and he buys two houses. I was pretty damn excited about it all, but he didn't ask me to move in with him. He started to talk about a couple of guys he may ask to be his roommates. I couldn't even hide my anger. We've been together for two years, I want to marry him, and he isn't even sure he wants me to move in with him. He didn't say it, but talking about roommates is the same thing as saying it. I told him straight, that if he didn't ask me to move in, we were done. It's embarrassing. Over two years together and he wants to turn his new place into a bachelor pad? I'd rather be alone than be that girl. So he asked me to move in. I should have felt bad about giving him an ultimatum. But I didn't. He should have felt bad about putting me into that situation in the first place. Just when I thought we were getting somewhere, I get slapped in the face with the reality that I am on thin ice with him. That our commitment could fall apart at any moment. I know I have to step it up at the new place. Keep things tidier. Be more like his mother and his sister. I hate doing the Betty Sue homemaker thing, but I'll do it at the new place. The excitement I feel about getting out of my trailer, I can't contain it. I'm finally close to having a life worth bragging about again. Worth being proud of. I just want to live life unashamed of my home. To be able to give my address out freely, without worrying that the person I'm giving it to will know I'm in a trailer park on the north side. It always comes back to this. The same shame.

I thought about the boys who had made fun of me, called me trash in school. The same boys who wanted me as an adult.

The one who pushed himself inside of me three years ago. I still haven't told anyone. I still haven't figured out what that was.

IT HAPPENED OVER THE SUMMER, the first time I shook. The first time I trembled. Connor and I were in bed, touching and tasting. We were tender one moment, rough the next. He pinned my arms above my head, ran his tongue down my throat, and I moaned.

When he touched me, I forgot other men. I forgot other half lovers and leavers. I forgot who I was.

But that hot night was different. The window next to my bed was open, I could hear a car alarm going off in the trailer park. My skin was sweaty, slick.

My moan turned into a whimper. A salty tear fell down my cheek and I pulled away from Connor.

I was a hot coil, wound tight.

I had found myself day dreaming at work, boiling over. I still worked on the sales floor from time to time, despite my promotion. When white haired men would watch me walk by, a sickness took root in my belly. I couldn't find a name or a word for the feeling I got. But a seed was planted, and I started to wonder. To pull at the recesses of my mind.

It was there on the fringes. I just needed to reach out.

Connor pulled away from me, worry woven into his brow. "Are you okay? What's wrong?"

He pulled me to him and I wept. It was the first time I let the dam break, but it wasn't the first time I wanted to pull away from him.

I had triggers. Arms pinned, nipples rose and wet from his tongue. Things that had turned me on, now turned my belly sour.

I didn't say much that night. I let him pull it out a little.

"Did someone do something to you?"

It occurred to me then that he had seen my turning before, the way I had started to dull myself.

"I think so," I whispered, to his chest, to his heart.

WHEN YOUR INNOCENCE DIES, sometimes, you barely see it. I couldn't see it. It was shrouded in mist and the mind is a masterful thing. I couldn't pull any memory up. I went back and forth, questioning myself. Half believing and half damning my own heart.

I barely talked to my stepfather. What would I lose by writing him out completely? I would be the bad daughter, the bad sister. Could I risk all of that on a memory that I couldn't even pull up?

In the fall, my mother came by my work. She was getting lunch nearby and wanted to talk to me.

"You remember your cousin Arya in Miami?"

"Yes," I replied, pulling one of her fries from her plate. We were sitting in the lounge, where our customers could go sit when they stopped in off the interstate.

I didn't know my cousin. I hadn't seen her since we moved to Missouri in 1992. I was nine when I left Florida. Arya was a year younger than me. She was a cruel little girl, much like her mother, who was my stepfather's sister.

One day my mother had to pick me up from their house because I was crying. Arya had told me I didn't even have a dad, that her uncle didn't even want me. I had learned just two months prior that the man I thought was my father was not in fact my father. He had come into my life at such a young age, I didn't know him as anything else.

"She's saying your stepfather did something to her." My mom took a bite of her burger, looked me in the eye.

My heart thundered in my chest. I wanted to spit out the fry that was in my mouth, but I couldn't give myself away. I wasn't ready. I couldn't ruin my mother's world.

"Oh yeah?" I swallowed, reached for her drink. I should have felt relief, knowing I wasn't crazy. I didn't make anything up. Instead, I felt a hollow hole in my chest start to open up. *I was not the only one he hurt.*

My mother and stepfather moved us to Missouri to escape the big cities, the crime, the drugs. I learned that Arya had fallen into some of those traps. Miami was blamed, but what about the man? What about the man who hurt her? The one who hurt me?

When I got home that night, I told Connor what I had learned.

He never questioned me, not the way I questioned myself. He took my words as truth, saw the reality written on my face, felt it in my shaking limbs.

He believed me, but he ended up failing me, too.

43

RESENTMENT

"How would he fail you?"

I find a worn spot on the cover of the journal in front of me, press my thumb into it, and think of all the ways. "He didn't know how to talk to me back then. He would change, eventually, but it took me leaving to do that."

"What couldn't he talk to you about?" She knows, but this is her way.

"What my stepfather did. Or, not what he did, how it made me feel. He couldn't understand my grief, the lack of rage. That would come, later, but I wasn't there yet. I mourned the loss of the only father I knew. I remembered the good times. When he would play games in the living room with my me and my brother. It was like someone had died. It was more than a memory dying. He was dying inside of me, and who I was, she was dying, too."

"It's hard for people who haven't been abused to understand it."

I don't want to understand, I am pulled back to all the resentment I had for Connor. "I know. He wanted anger. I didn't have it yet. And when I did, Connor was the first one to get it. For not understanding. For not knowing how to make me feel better."

44

JUST SAD

I FEEL like I'm running in a vat of glue. I am stuck and still. I can't move. Confessions are supposed to set you free, right? Especially when you haven't done something wrong? Sometimes I wonder how everyone in my life would carry on without me. How easily it would go. My employer would hire someone from the stack of applications on the front counter. My friends would mourn for a while, but eventually, my seat at the bar would be filled. My family would cry to one another. They would keep living. Connor would find someone new to love. Someone who didn't have ugly things to tell him in the dark of her bedroom. I just couldn't do it anymore. I couldn't keep flinching when he touched me. I couldn't hide it. He tensed when I tensed. We mirrored each other and the lump in my throat was getting so hard to choke down. I wanted to die. I would have taken that over speaking my truth out loud, making it real.

LIFE DID NOT CARE for your plans. I saw that now.

I had a new home. And it felt like a home. A two-story white house. Red shutters. Crown molding. Hardwood floors.

I said goodbye to my trailer, didn't look back. I felt a peace wash over me when I walked into my new home after a long day at work. A slow peace, a fading peace, a peace that could not last.

My life was a paper life, easily crumbled, often ripped.

Connor was rarely home. He worked all day, then went over to the other house he bought, the fixer-upper. He wanted to bring in extra income, turn it into a rental. But he didn't have a lot of extra money to hire someone to do all the work. His family offered, but taking gifts from them hurt his pride. He wanted the life they had, but he wanted to build it for himself. It was one of the things I admired about him. The way he worked.

Now, that trait in him that I admired, was hurting me.

DEPRESSION, much like anxiety, was a foreign word to me back then. We didn't talk about those things. My family never did. My friends never did. If you were down, you were just sad. No one spoke of a deeper meaning.

I was falling deeper and deeper into a hole that I feared I would not be able to crawl out of. Only one person knew what my stepfather did to me. Connor. And he was never home, never around.

Maybe he didn't want to see the way I was losing weight, losing the color in my face.

The weight of my secret was eating at me. I was making it all up, I knew, but it was still real.

No one expected me to keep in touch with my stepfather that often. So when I decided to write him out of my life, the world did not shift. No one alerted the press. The alarm was all in my head, eating away.

Then, the call came. It was a Thursday night, and I was lying in bed. Our house still wasn't fully put together. There was only so much I could do with the bigger pieces without Connor to help. We had just bought a new bed two days before, and it was downstairs in our living room.

I had drawn all the shades, was lying in clean sheets after a shower when I heard the ringing.

"Gwen," my mother said, as if she didn't know she called me.

I rolled my eyes and sighed. "Yes." I was on the defense, afraid she would scold me for my silence toward my stepfather. She always had a way of knowing those things. When she told me what Arya said, that he molested her, I didn't see damnation in her eyes. Despite all he did to my mother, the cheating, the lies, she still supported him. It made me resent her, I could see that now.

"Have you talked to your father?"

It was a question I heard time and time again. I was twenty-nine years old and here she was, still trying to make our relationship more than it was. Always calling my brother and I, urging us to reach out to him. Why did we, the children, have to be the bigger person? It made me rebel, ignore his number on my phone.

"No," I said, clipped, pissed. I propped myself up on my elbow and reached for the light switch above my head, my hand still when she spoke again.

"He's sick. He has cancer."

I DID NOT WANT to cry when I got the news, but I did. I wasn't sure who for. For myself? For him? I knew I had to choke on my secret. I couldn't come out then, accuse him of molesting me if he was dying.

I couldn't stomach the other hurt there. I hurt in the pits of myself. *I didn't want him to die. I wanted him to die.* No one tells you how to feel when your monster is melting away.

I didn't want to see him again, but I would have to. I would have to go to the hospital.

I would have to smile at him and hug him and let him put his hands on me, the ones that changed me, the ones that broke me.

45

I WAS SILENT

Connor

THERE IS something inside of me, in my blood, that wants to go off on her. I held her as she shook the night she told me she thought someone had molested her. The signs had been there for a while. She was pulling away when we slept together. She had always been a spirited lover. We loved to play. My hand around her neck, reverse cowgirl, fucking on the hood of her little Hyundai. All summer she had been timid. She rarely slept. I would wake in the night, in her tiny trailer, alone in bed. I would look for her every time, and find her the same way every time.

She would be at her dining room table, with a pad of paper, scribbling away. *I couldn't sleep. I'm sorry, babe. Did I wake you?* would often be what tumbled from her mouth. I would take her hand, pull her up, wrap myself around her.

Sometimes, she came to me. Sometimes, she insisted I try to fall asleep again.

Gwen loved to write in a journal. It never really interested me much, the contents of those pages, until I was losing her. Until her secrets no longer reached my ears. I didn't know her sleepless nights would be the first nail in our coffin. I couldn't reach her. I couldn't understand her. So I was silent. I was a wall and she flowed around me.

The day she told me she wanted to go see her stepfather in the hospital, the one who violated her, I didn't argue. I let a bitter seed bloom into something resentful in my stomach. *How could she go see him? How could she still care about him?*

She told me to keep quiet about what happened to her. She couldn't remember it anyway, and her family couldn't know. So I was without a confidant. No one to confess my feelings to. No one but her and I couldn't burden her. She was dealing with enough. Weight loss. Hair loss. Her blue eyes were grey and her skin seemed to change color before my eyes.

This was supposed to be one of the best times of our lives. I had bought a house. We were out of her tiny trailer. I was working a lot, but I hoped my goals made her happy. I knew she wanted to marry me but I wasn't ready. We needed to build something together. To build a foundation. Financially and emotionally. Money was on our side but this would be the beginning of the slip. I didn't know it then, but a pit was pooling around our feet. We would rise some days, but we would always be our past. If I had known our rocky beginnings would be better than our future, would I still have tried? Hard to say.

There was this pull I felt.

Always toward Gwen.

Even when I hated her, I felt it.

I LOVED THE LIE

So much time has slipped by, so easily, and sad. So sad like me, all the time. It's May now and I don't know where the time has gone. The new house looks great. My stepfather is in stable condition, so I don't have to go see him in the hospital. I don't have to pretend. I can just hide away, go on with life. I have a new friend now anyway, someone to distract me from the fact that Connor and I aren't what we used to be. You can find friends in the strangest of places.

Just before Connor and I got together, last year, he was seeing a girl. I knew her. The redhead.

Her brother and my brother lived together. We went to the same school but with her being six years younger than me, it's not like we could hang out or anything.

When I found out Connor was hanging out with her back then I saw red. Not red like her hair, red like rage. Another redhead was getting in between us.

She wasn't the bad penny but she was a wedge in my way. When a coworker told me she was hanging with a girlfriend and asked me to come along I showed little interest. When she told me that Kate, the red-headed wedge from last year, would be there, I decided to go.

I wanted to be petty. To rub it in her face that I had Connor, even though that didn't seem like anything to brag about anymore. I liked to win and I could be ugly.

When I got into the car with the girls, I kept quiet. I didn't have a game plan for my childish release. I wanted to feel her out. I didn't expect to have more fun with Kate that night than the girl I worked with.

I don't often click with women. I don't often click with anyone, actually. There was something about Kate's easy laugh. It was loud and warm. She said she hated it, that it embarrassed her, but I liked it. I liked people who were open and talkative. I was the opposite and those were the people who always drew me out.

I abandoned my plan to be petty. I talked to her about our brothers and our hometown. We exchanged numbers and we avoided the fact that if anyone knew we were friends they would think it was a lie, a joke.

When I got home I told Connor how much I liked Kate. I think it made him uncomfortable, and maybe he questioned Kate's motives for being my friend.

Women are expected to hate each other over men. And we often do. I went out into the night with a hate in my heart. A possessiveness over my boyfriend, but it was driven away by kindness. I never made a snide remark. They all drowned in my throat when confronted with honesty and an open mind.

Sometimes you meet someone and they reflect in your good qualities. I needed to lay down my fighting tools. Connor was mine. But I doubted any commitment made to me these days. Marriages fell apart. Families fell apart. How could we not?

I wanted to marry Connor, despite our issues. I wanted a little bit more security.

I was always craving that. Security. Though, I wasn't sure what I would do with it.

MY SUSPICIONS WERE CONFIRMED when I started to tell people that Kate and I were friends. Lesley rejected the idea. Said she was out to get me. I wanted to ask her how she knew. If she recognized a likeness since she was the shittiest friend I ever had.

Maybe she was afraid I would see someone with honest intentions and leave her, drop her.

If we didn't work together, I would have done it a long time ago. But I felt married to the idea that we needed to get along.

It took a while for Connor to ease into the idea as well. When the three of us finally hung out, I felt no jealousy when Kate and Connor talked. They acted more like brother and sister than two people who had slept together. It was no wonder they didn't work out.

I would never have expected that we would all live together later.

It wasn't too much later that Lesley found another job. As soon as she was gone we stopped talking. We deleted each other from Facebook. I finally felt like I had someone else on my side. Maybe I could eventually tell a friend about what I was feeling, what was hurting me, and I could feel better.

I loved the lie.

47

A CHILD OF MY OWN

"IT WASN'T LONG before I started to realize that I didn't recognize myself. I had bitten my tongue so many times I was surprised it hadn't fallen off into my mouth. I deserved to choke on the blood. I changed myself too much for Connor, and never told him the fear I had over my morphing skin, that all I had in my palms for him was resentment. I was reading a lot. So many stories of girls and guys who couldn't get their love figured out because they couldn't communicate. It was infuriating. I wanted to throw books across the room, scream at them."

"Because that's the life you were living?"

"Yes. I knew what it was like to watch your face fall in reflected glass. To watch words die in your own eyes. I wanted to keep Connor, above all else. I didn't care how I lost myself in the meantime. He could settle down with my corpse. The shell of the feisty woman I used to be."

"Did anyone point out the changes in you?"

"No. The world wants the wild girls to settle down. Get married. Have kids. I was on the path to being what society needed me to be. One person noticed. Kate. We were supportive of each other, but we knew our boundaries. Where our opinions were not necessary.

Or where they would be met with regret. It was enough to have a friend there who supported me unconditionally. She would be there if I stayed or if I left. If she knew just how sad I was maybe she would have pressed more. But I was so skilled at hiding my lifeless eyes. At lying in texts."

"But not face-to-face. You say you can't hide your emotions. And I can see that."

"Yeah. I don't know if it's a blessing or a curse." I pause. "My mother always told me to be a strong woman. But I watched her bend herself into a half-woman for my stepfather. For the man who hurt me. Then I watched her do it again and again. I wonder if it started with my biological father. Was it a learned skill? To break your mold and let yourself spill all over the floor for a man? Did she learn it from her mother? I had never seen my grandfather be anything but kind, but, do we truly know anyone? Ever?"

"What happens behind closed doors is often hidden. You just said you hid what was going on between you and Connor. What was his family like?"

"Perfect," I laugh, and it is not happy. "I was so envious of Connor's family. But they made him the way he was. Connor with the stoic face. With the heart of stone. Never letting his feelings out."

"Did you try to talk to him?"

"No. I think our beginning caused us to hide our feelings from each other. We trained ourselves to be that way. To hide the truth. He couldn't wrap his head around the fact that I didn't want to tell anyone about what my father did. But how could he? He was untouched, from this Hallmark Card life. He couldn't relate to that and I resented him for not being able to open his eyes to the way things were tearing me apart. It was then, in his silence, that I turned to words."

"What did you write?"

"My first novel. When Connor was silent for days at a time, I wrote my story. The one he could never sit down to hear out, fully. I made up a girl, named her Sera, a name I had reserved for a little girl I hoped to one day have. And I made her story just as mine. My mother still didn't know she had married a monster. My brother didn't know his father was sick. Not just with cancer, with a sick attraction to little girls. I wanted one of those things to kill him. I wanted so many dark things. In those days, I started to lose more than gain."

"What was the hardest thing to lose?"

"My desire to have a child of my own."

48

INVISIBLE CLOCK

Connor

I'VE NEVER UNDERSTOOD the men who told their girlfriends or wives that they couldn't go out and have fun. I wasn't controlling in that way, and neither was Gwen. We never had to ask permission to do anything and we never told each other no. If she wanted to go out with her friends, then she could go out with her friends and the same kindness was extended to me. I was working late a lot. And often, whenever I came home, she would be out with her friends. I didn't expect her to just wait around for me. But it was lonely coming home to an empty house all the time.

There was nothing wrong with her friends necessarily, but they were single, and their idea of having fun was different than what I hoped hers would be. I knew the way guys looked at her. And there was no way they weren't still looking at her that way. It shouldn't have mattered how men looked at her. All that mattered was how she was looking at them. The truth was, she pulled away. I feared she was unhappy. The harder truth to face was that I didn't blame her.

Sometimes every little thing you complain about in someone is every little thing you love about them. You don't realize that you're changing them, that you want them to stand up to you.

Gwen was once fiery, dominant, in the early days. She wasn't anymore. She had bowed down to something inside of me that she saw, something I couldn't change her view on. I never wanted to control her. But she had taken into consideration everything I wanted and was throwing away her own wants for me.

Sometimes it was something small and simple like a TV show she wanted to watch and I knew she wanted to watch it, but when I came home and she had ESPN on for me, I wouldn't say anything. I would just wait to see what she would do and she would never use her voice. She turned into a tiny meek mouse.

If I was being honest with myself, I loved the way our mistakes looked in past tense. They were neat and tidy. Easy to attach solutions to. I was too caught up in perfect. That was my problem. One of them.

There was an invisible clock in my heart. One that counted down to the day I would propose to Gwen. It would start over every time she lashed out. Every time she fell into a pit. Every time she went weeks without sweeping our kitchen floor. Every time she showed her biting jealousy.

Perfection. That's what I wanted. I didn't see it at the time, but I would when she left me.

I would never be able to break her of her reach for perfection. I planted it there. It was a stain between us.

She was never enough for me, not in her eyes, because I strung her along for so long. I wish we could have gone back to the beginning. Before we both fucked it up.

49

A BIGGER MONSTER

"When I was fifteen, I wrote poetry about a boy I had a crush on. He was a mean popular kid, but I was fifteen and I didn't care. I didn't know then that it would be a pattern, to love boys who were mean to me. When I started writing again as an adult, it was to subdue the sadness I had inside. I wrote about Connor. All the things we could never say to each other's faces. I pretended the typewriter I bought was for show. A new prop for the house.

"Our home was decorated in warm colors. I started working on it when I was warmer. Nothing inside our home back then matched my inside. I want stark white, nothingness. The black typewriter would look beautiful in a white room with nothing but a blue desk. But no, my house was warm reds and tans, a constant reminder of the days when I had hope. That he would marry me and we would create a family here. I kept the typewriter in my office. I typed away when Connor was gone on business trips for his new job. I stashed the little papers I typed in a box behind the file cabinet."

"Were you afraid of what he would realize if he read your words?"

"Yes. He would see the truth. He barely looked into my eyes back then. When he came home, I didn't hug him. I didn't kiss him. And he didn't complain. I said 'hello' and 'how was your trip' and his monotone voice filled the space between us. It was vapor, stagnant."

"What did you do with the words you wrote on those little papers?"

"I never thought about posting my poems online. It seemed like a stupid idea. When I was a little girl, I wanted to be a lot of things – an actress, a vet, a writer, a poet. I let my dreams slip away because my anxiety was a bigger monster than they were. It crashed into the room of my heart and soul and left no room for the things I desired.

Connor had been gone for a five-day trip when I posted a piece online for the first time. Having it go viral was not in the cards. I had already been working on my first novel for years. I was getting nowhere. The story was too big, too personal. I modeled my character after myself and that was a mistake. It was the only way to tell the story of what my stepfather had done to me, but I couldn't work my way through it. I put it aside for months at a time. I picked a pseudonym from the beginning. Something to hide behind. When I posted my poem, I used that same name. Then I saw it spreading across the internet like wildfire. Every day more people followed my new poetry social media account no one knew about. Not Kate. Not my mother. Not Connor. I was too embarrassed to tell them. It was too raw, the words I was posting."

"But that made it easier, right? To hide behind the name?"

"Yes. How could that ever be the real me? Posting my feelings online when I wouldn't dare utter to them to the man who was supposed to love me more than anyone in the world? The man who ignored me, left the room when family asked when we were going to finally get married?"

"Maybe things would have been different if you had opened up to him then."

I laugh. "Yes, maybe, but he didn't deserve to see my secrets. I trusted strangers with them more than him. They couldn't use them or wound me. But he didn't need random words typed on a paper to wound me. He did it best in his absence. His silence. I should have never moved in. I missed my trailer and the freedom I felt there. I missed knowing that no matter how much someone hurt me, I could just shut them out, turn off my phone, lock my doors. I didn't have that escape there, in the home we shared. I did on the days Connor was gone, but when he was home it was a delicate balancing act. A tightrope tango. Pretending nothing was wrong. Crying in the shower, hoping he wouldn't hear."

"You really think he didn't see how unhappy you were?"

"I know he did. He told me later, after I left him. How do two people become so lost from each other? So distant? Maybe he looked at me differently. It had been over two years since I told him about the abuse right before we moved in together. Was it the truth that drove the wedge between us? Was it living together? Were we simply just not a good match?"

"Do you believe sometimes it just comes down to that? Two people who love each other but are just not a good match? What about work? It sounds like neither of you were putting in the work."

"You're right. We weren't. But I couldn't go, yet. For all the ice I had around me, I couldn't handle the thought of leaving him alone. I would bury myself in a grave of loneliness and despair if it meant he wouldn't hurt. Is that love? That kind of sacrifice? I didn't want to be the woman who sacrificed herself for others. I wanted to be as selfish as I damned myself for being."

"Do you still damn yourself for being selfish?"

"Yes. And him, too. I was too afraid to be without him so I let us live this gross lie, he did it ,too. He felt it, I knew. He wouldn't let go either. Maybe we deserved each other and that brutal torment."

"What was your biggest fear?"

"Becoming one of them. Every woman I saw, the ones I pitied. In a loveless marriage, loathing their partner. I was no better than those I damned."

BLOOMED

I KNOW I'm doing it. I know I am self-sabotaging, but I can't stop. Today, this week, this moment, I feel suffocated. I started drinking again. Blacking out. I forget Connor when I'm out. I force myself to forget him. Too many Christmases have gone by with no proposal. Too many Valentine's Days. I don't want to start my forever with him on a cliché day, but I would take it. I would take it on any day, just as long as he was asking me. We've been together for four years. I'm thirty-one and this is not where I expected us to be. I turn to the bottle and the page more than the man I love, the man who supposedly loves me.

I look back at our story and I cry. I have had to force him into everything. Into a relationship. Into living together. I can't force him to go buy a ring, and I don't want to be that girl. I've finally had enough. And as usual, instead of telling him I've had enough, I retreat. Into myself, into the page. Into the black.

THE MESSAGES FILLED my inbox almost instantly. Girls who had been through what I had been through. Shared pain. Matching scars. Girls who hadn't named their abuser. Who hadn't uttered a word. They were all there, bundled together, holding hands through my computer screen, reaching for me.

I cringed at the thought of my family finding my writing, learning the truth that way. I needed to come clean, but I was not ready.

The only person who knew in my real life had distanced himself so far from me, I barely recognized him.

One person who reached out stood out to me amongst all the faces.

He was beautiful, completely not my type. His hair was long, grazing his shoulders, and he was blonde. My mother always hated blondes. I inherited her distaste. But this man, he was different. I found myself drawn to him. To his Instagram account. He was a writer as well. He wrote about a pain I knew. The bitter pain of not wanting to be alive some days. His style, the stop and start of his stanzas, it reeled me in. I was just as fascinated by his words as I was by his lips, his eyes. I couldn't tell the color in his black and white photo. But I wanted to know it, to know him.

I found myself dreaming about him, wondering what his voice sounded like. I convinced myself it was harmless, but I knew better.

I told myself it was sort of like developing a crush on a celebrity you saw on a screen. I ignored the message from him in my inbox for two weeks. Then I caved.

We talked about little things. Where we lived. Our favorite writers. Our shared admiration for each other's style. He was younger than me, and that made me pause, made me think our conversations were dangerous.

I find something so beautiful, nonthreatening about a younger man. As if a man younger than me hadn't grown into his killing tools. As if my years on him served as an armor. I felt the thing I needed most, felt it in my bones, my sighs and slow stretch of my teeth grazing my lip when I stared at his photo. *Control*.

I didn't have it. I knew it wasn't true. I knew deep down, that a younger man could hurt me just the way men my age could.

But I liked to lie to myself. I liked to pretend this was a game I could come out on top of.

When he asked for my number, I gave it to him. He wanted to talk about writing. Wanted to write some poetry together. My friends, single friends, told me about the immature boys sending them dick pics. God, if a guy really wanted to get a girl going, he would send her some poetry into her inbox, that would do the trick.

When Logan sent me his words, I withered, then bloomed.

It is a slow death and birth, those moments lasted minutes, hours, days.

I came alive in ways I never thought possible.

We never texted late at night. He told me about a concert he was going to and I told him about my job. I was so careful not to cross a line that I knew I was crossing. A line I crossed by just thinking about going over the edge, falling into something I could not recover from.

Connor volunteered for more work trips. I spent my birthday alone and I got no flowers, no gift. Just a promise for a dinner date when he was back in town.

I hoped he would forget, and checked the bathroom mirror for more wrinkles.

Logan asked me my age and I didn't lie to him. He asked if he could call me so I ignored him for two weeks.

A brutal imbalance threatened my body. I stopped eating, developed a rash on my neck, my stress and broken heart too overwhelming. I stopped sleeping and wrote more in a month than I had in the past ten years. Everything was painted in my loneliness and my remorse. My longing for Logan and my resentment for Connor. I reached for him under the covers when he was home and he was always asleep, or pretending to be asleep. The shower was the only place I knew to go to. My tears mingled with the shower stream. I told Kate about my new friend and she asked to see what he looked like.

When she saw, she knew my secret. She knew my lie.

51

THE MOTHER OF MY CHILDREN

Connor

HOLIDAYS WERE ALWAYS tense for Gwen. My family would ask why we weren't married yet and I would brush the question away. It wasn't anyone's business and I wasn't sure it would work.

Gwen felt worse. I could see it on her face. How could she know when we would get married? She was waiting for me to ask her. Waiting in vain, maybe. Once, a friend was brought up in conversation, a friend who quit her job to stay at home with her kids. Gwen said she would want to work still. I told her that I wanted the mother of my children to stay home with my kids. When I look back now, I could see it was the way I said it. *The mother of my children.* I didn't say her.

This past Christmas, her tune changed. She was being quiet in the car on the way home. I asked her why her tongue was still in her mouth, and she dropped a tiny truth. It didn't feel like a bomb then, but it would mar us, leave us decimated.

She said she wasn't sure she wanted kids anymore. We hadn't talked about it much, and some days I wasn't sure when or if I would be ready either, but it was one more thing to add to my list.

The way I drove her away, it was slow. Never deliberate. It was my pursuit of a perfection that could not be achieved. I see that now.

PART OF MYSELF

"I DID TRY. I did try to fight it."

"Your attraction to Logan?"

"More than that. I tried to fight knowing him. To fight seeing inside of his heart. But the more I read his writing, the more I knew. I knew I couldn't stay away. It all built up, for a couple of months, until one night he wanted to call me. I was out of town on business, and free to hear his voice. So I said yes. I said yes, and lost part of myself. I've never been able to get it back."

I'M NOT SUPPOSED TO FEEL THIS WAY

"WE SHOULDN'T BE TALKING," I mumbled.

"I know. This is so strange though. I like the way your voice sounds."

"I like the way your voice sounds, too." I felt it in my belly.

"We don't have to talk if you don't want to. I can hang up. You can hang up," he said. I heard hope laced into the words. He didn't want that. I didn't want that.

"I don't want to though," I said, voicing our thoughts, the guilt punching me in the gut.

"Where are you?"

"My hotel room," I said. "I'm done for the day. I go home in a couple of days."

"Do you travel for work often?"

"Kind of," I replied. I liked that part of my job. When I was away from my home, when I was away from Connor's silence, able to sit in a room and write my ache away.

I looked over at my typewriter. I had loaded it into the car before I left, needing my constant friend. The one who kept my secrets.

"The thing I told you earlier. Not many people know it. You're one of four people. I don't know why I told you. I just feel like, I don't know, like you know me." He was hushed.

"I feel that way, too. I don't know what to do with it. It makes me sad." My words dripped honestly.

"Why?"

"Because I'm not supposed to feel this way. Not for you, anyway." I wanted Connor to be the one confessing, letting me confess without judgment. But he couldn't stop playing that role. The one who damned me. With his dark silence, his dark eyes.

"We are often caught between what we are supposed to feel and what we feel. The true way we feel," he said.

"I guess. I don't really like myself right now." It was true. My desire was swirling under my skin. My want was apparent. My skin was flushed.

"I'm sorry. I don't want to make you feel guilty." He didn't sound sorry.

"I think you want to make me feel this way," I said. And I meant it. He wanted to know I felt the same way he did.

"Fuck," he sighed. "I wish I could see your face right now. Let me FaceTime you."

"No. That's too much. This is bad as it is."

I wanted to hang up. To lose his number. Instead, I pulled the covers up higher, under my chin. I shivered in the hotel room. My toes were sweating in my heavy socks. It was a chilly February. Even colder back home, up north, where Connor was.

He told me he would call me after he finished dinner, that was two hours ago. He forgot. As usual. I could have called him, asking what was up. But often I let him let me down. I didn't want to fight for his attention, for his affections and love, not anymore. I had given up a while ago. I wasn't even sure when we had laughed with each other last.

I felt like a Stepford wife. Except I was no wife and I was shit at the housework. I was just a robot who occupied space. My half of the bed, my loveseat. I was wasting that space.

Some other girl could fill it, fill Connor's heart, where I was failing to. Maybe she would be perfect in all the ways he needed a woman to be.

I was so tired of the trying. To be the perfect daughter, the perfect friend, lover, coworker, and artist. I felt stretched thin. Ready to break under the pressure.

I liked sitting in this hotel room, just existing. Just walking and not feeling like I was saying all the wrong things. Like I was the fool.

"Where did you grow up?" I asked.

"Tennessee."

I coughed and nearly dropped the phone. I was going to Tennessee the next day, to meet up with Kate. She had moved away to Nashville and I missed her. My work trip was bringing me close enough to go see her, to drink with her, and to forget.

"Where in Tennessee?" I said, the shock bubbling over.

"Knoxville. About two hours from Nashville."

"That's where I'm heading tomorrow night. It's my favorite city."

"I love Nashville. I used to go there all the time with my college friends."

College wasn't too long ago for him, he was only twenty-five. God. I stared at the ceiling. Zeroed in on the smoke alarm across the room. I heard Logan clear his throat.

"Are you still there?" he asked.

"I wish I knew you in real life," I said. Armor falls at the worst moments for me.

"Me too," he replied.

I loved his soft voice. It felt safe. My anxiety wasn't set off by the tone of his voice, by his words. I imagined him reciting his poetry to me in a dark room.

"This feels like a cruel trick," he said.

"I agree. I think I kind of wish I never messaged you back. I'm sorry. I hope you don't take that the wrong way." Life would be simpler in black and white, cruel greys. He was color.

"I'm not. I'm sorry I'm messing your life up. Or confusing you. I guess that was presumptuous."

I didn't like arrogant men, not anymore. I wanted someone soft. Someone to soften me. "My life was a mess before I met you. I think you're just making me say out loud all the things I never could."

"Like what?"

"That I am unhappy with my life. I've known that for a while. But I've never said it out loud."

"You can say anything out loud to me."

I believed him.

I DID NOT REACH FOR HER

Connor

SOMETIMES SHE WOULD ASK me why I loved her. It was always hard to answer. I could sit down and write out reasons. Superficial reasons. She was beautiful. There was no one beautiful to me the way she was. It was like someone had made her for me. Five years together, and never once was there a part of me that didn't desire her. I loved her, I hated her. I wanted to leave her, I wanted to pin her down. Through everything, I wanted her, deep in the pit of me. I would have grown old with her. Toward the end, she became self-conscious. Over the wrinkles beginning to form around her eyes. Over the ten pounds she gained. She told me she gained it but I never saw it. I saw her lose the weight at the end. It should have been a smoke signal, but I had long stopped seeing her cries for help.

I never was able to give her that answer. The why of my love. Maybe that's why she left. She wanted a list. But her hands, on a list, were deadly. She wanted to dissect it. To scribble all over the pages. To show me why I shouldn't love her. Because she never felt like she deserved it. She always wanted to push me to leave. So she could be right. She was convinced that every man wanted to leave her. It's hard to get over the crimes our parents make against us. I never knew that pain. I had a perfect family. Something she loved to use as a weapon against me.

We had too many weapons behind our backs, ready to pull out.

IN OUR LIVING room sat a full-size couch and a loveseat. The couch was where I spent my time, the loveseat was where Gwen spent hers. When we moved in together, we shared the couch. We held each other. We cuddled on Sundays. Now there's a void between us.

It was a Friday night when it happened. I came home late from work, and she was on the loveseat. A blanket around her, laptop in her lap. She barely looked up when I walked in the door.

Tomorrow was Valentine's Day. I had made no plans. No flowers were coming. She didn't care about big shows. We were past that.

I went upstairs and took a shower. When I came downstairs, she looked up from her work, a novel she had been tinkering with for years.

"How was your day?" It was barely a question. More of a habit. Something she was required to ask.

"Fine. Yours?" I could dance the dance, too. I grabbed a beer from the fridge and sat down. It was then that I noticed the glass of wine on the coffee table. It was empty. I looked up at her face, her cheeks were red.

The initial moment we ended it was very anticlimactic. But we were so numb to each other for so long, I had no reason to expect raised voices, a fight.

She sat up, closed her laptop, and stared at the coffee table. Her hands were a tight knot in her lap.

"What is it?" I asked her, but I knew it already. I could feel it in the air. I would tell her later, how I could feel her. Miles away, I could feel her sadness. I would learn to be open, open to my heart and the feelings in there. But it was too late. Her leaving, it would break me.

"I'm not happy. And I don't think you are either." Her voice was cold, flat. I'd never heard it that way. Lifeless and resolute.

I pulled my hands up, ran them through my short hair. "I'm not." There was no use in lying. That wasn't my style. I would later learn it was hers.

"So, what do we do?" she asked.

"I think you know what you want to do." I looked up, into her eyes. How long had it been since I had done that? "Right?"

She cried, and I did not reach for her. I just let her go upstairs to pack a bag.

55

I'M SAVING YOU

IT WAS the expectations that killed me, killed us. When are you getting married? When are you having kids? My life wasn't enough. I was being weighed and measured, whether I wanted to be or not. It was sad but other people can steal the magic from the things you once wanted more than anything. I'm not sure if it was society's expectations or Connor's lack of care for the things that I wanted that hurt me the most, behind the abuse, which was the biggest killer of all my little girl dreams. I didn't want to avoid holidays anymore. I knew which people would ask about my bare ring finger and my flat belly if I ran into them at Walmart, so I ducked down aisles. The asking did slow though, quelled by too many sharp words or the constant disappointing answers from me.

I'd convinced myself fairytales were shit, honestly. I would hang art in my trailer, in the places I had saved on the wall, and in my heart, for beautiful photos of our ghost children, our make-believe wedding day. If you despair, turn to art. It is constant, likes the waves. Always changing but salty and never one to fade away. Never to fade away like my feelings for Connor. I felt resentment. I was a shell of the woman I was, or the woman thought I would become.

IN MY LAST week at the house, Connor changed. He started to reject the decision I thought we had mutually agreed upon.

"Maybe we can work this out. Maybe you can go to therapy?"

I was kneeling over a box, placing books inside. "I need to go to therapy now?"

"You don't think it would help?"

"Of course, that's the answer, right? Send me to therapy. Because you're perfect. Always so perfect." My voice was not raised. I spoke into the box, to the faces of the books, not to Connor's face. I couldn't look at it anymore. It was breaking me.

"You've been depressed, for, I don't even know how long." His voice was sad and I didn't know what to do with that, after years of no life in it.

I cut him off. "I have been. And you left me alone." *Alone to fall for someone else.*

"I didn't know what to say to you."

"So you said nothing? Babe," I stopped. I didn't know how to say his name. The endearment fell out. "I'm sorry. I just, I didn't mean to call you that."

"It's okay."

I breathed in. "Connor, you left me alone too much. Please don't make me say things to hurt you." I pushed up from the floor, turned to him. He was standing in the kitchen doorway. I had boxes stacked everywhere in the dining room.

"What could you possibly say that would hurt me more than you leaving me?"

"I don't want to have kids anymore. It's not just a doubt anymore, it's a truth." I started to cry, and it was an ugly sound. His body leaned forward, pulled like a magnet to my pain, when for years, it pushed. "Don't," I said, putting my right palm up. "Don't hug me. Don't do those things now, when you couldn't do them when we were together." I saw his lip trembling, the shaking of his fist, he tapped it against his thigh. "I'm not who I was when we got together. I don't want to get married anymore. I don't want to have kids. I don't want any of it. It all died inside of me. I don't know how to get it back out, but I know one thing for sure, and that's that I can't do it here. I can't be with someone I don't love anymore. I mean, I love you, I always fucking will, Connor, but I am not in love with you anymore. And I will not take away your chance to have a child. It's not your fault that I am this way now. I just want to be left alone in this. Okay? Can you just let me go? Let me be alone?"

"I don't know."

"You don't have a choice. I am not staying. I am saving both of us."

"You're killing me."

"No, I am setting you free to be with someone who will make you happy. Because honestly, you cannot convince me that these past few years have been happy. They haven't. We were roommates, not even friends."

"I know." He cannot argue, he cannot reach for me. He stared at the ceiling, instead, and let out an inhuman sound.

"You'll see it," I said, when the echo of his ache stopped reverberating off the walls. "I'm saving you."

PART IV

56

CRIME SCENE

"So you left Connor for Logan?"

"No." It wasn't that simple. "Other people assumed that, and no, I don't blame them. It looked that way. I had an emotional affair. Sure, I didn't meet Logan in person until I was single, living on my own, but the things we said, it was bad. I was ashamed of myself. It wasn't sexual, sexting and texting and all that. It was this emotional connection, I'd never experienced anything like it. He woke me up. How can you thank someone for that? I had been living my life in shades of grey, dull."

"Did he change you?"

"He made me feel alive again. Made me realize what I was doing to myself. I felt like I had lost the ability to sacrifice. I'd done it too often. I'd been a willing sacrifice for as long as I could remember."

"In what ways?"

"When I was a teenager, I guarded my virginity fiercely. Then I gave my sex away with a straight face and a twisted heart. I didn't want to do things the way other women did. I saw their faces and I wondered what they gave up. What their lives would be worth when they died. Would everything they gave up for others be worth it? I wanted a new leaf. I wanted to run away. But Connor was rooted there in Missouri. I resented him. He resented me. He says he didn't, but I knew he did. Or he would one day. It broke me to tell him the main reason I left him."

"And what was that?"

My chest feels like heavy bricks, a hot burning fire. I pull my hand to my throat, grace my collar bone with my pinky. "I didn't want to have a child anymore. I'd lost it, that wanting. My father stole it from me. Who would feed the baby when I was in the dark? On the days when I couldn't pull myself from our bed? He says it's as simple as just getting up and doing what needs to be done. But that's such an oversimplification of it."

"You said he couldn't relate to you. But he wanted you to be happy, right? Do you think that, deep down?"

"He wanted to seek his own happiness, through me. He never felt the cement, the quicksand. His veins were not filled with tar, like mine. He was made of good breeding, good intentions. He would be a good father, but what would they say of me? I was not his sister. I was not his mother. I was not kind and soft."

"Are you soft now?"

"Do I look soft?" We laugh. I push the hair from my face and lean on my forearms. "No, I am made of sharp edges. Would my child, our child, break herself on them? It was too much of a risk. That's what I told myself."

"What we feel isn't always the truth."

"Maybe, but it was my truth then. I saw all these people having child after child with no care in the world. No money to feed them. Why couldn't I worry a little less? For a while, I thought adoption would be the answer."

"Why did you change your mind then?"

"Just because I didn't have the child naturally doesn't mean he or she would be safe from me. I didn't worry I would physically hurt the child. I just worried I would be so cold, they would lack for warmth. And, would I resent the child? Would I regret the child?"

"It's hard to know until you're in it."

"Then it's too late, right? I am so vain." I look down at my hands, at the wrinkles in my knuckles. I don't look like the twenty-five-year-old girl from the beginning of this story, from ten years ago. "Would I look at my body like a crime scene?" I pause. "But then, I already do, don't I?"

LIKE LEGIT IN LOVE?

No one wants to talk about the women who are scared of commitment. It took me years to realize that I was one of them. I never wanted to get tangled in something I couldn't find my way out of. Marriage didn't scare me because you could always get a divorce. But having a child? You can't walk away from that kind of commitment. And what business did I have bringing life into this world when most days I didn't want to be alive myself? It's one of the many reasons I left Connor. It's one of the many reasons I've fallen for Logan. He doesn't ask me for anything I can't give. And he is just as broken as me.

THE SIX WEEKS following my breakup with Connor leading up to the first time I met Logan were some of the longest days of my life.

Connor insisted on helping me move. He bought brand new locks for all the doors of the abandoned trailer I returned to. He was worried about someone breaking in.

I found my old home in shambles. The yard was overrun. The long grass was spilling over like waves. I ignored it, no one wanted to get a lawnmower out in February.

The interior was covered in dust, the air was stale.

I brought too much back with me, the boxes were stacked above my head in the living room.

I had spent countless hours handpicking the items that decorated my home with Connor. I went to antique malls, swap meets, garage sales. I wanted everything to be unique. I wanted each piece to have had a life before coming into our home.

I couldn't leave it behind and I couldn't unpack it.

Every piece reminded me of my life with Connor, all the hope I once had in my heart, my aching ribs. I couldn't leave it either.

Connor's pain radiated off of him, pulsing. I didn't want to be near him. It hurt to see him that way. I was hoping for something easier.

When I broke up with him, he agreed with me, that it was the best thing to do. Then the next morning he woke up changed, desperate to have me back. He followed me from room to room. He didn't touch me, but his stare choked me.

I told him I was going back to my trailer and he argued. He said I should stay in the guest room until I found a more suitable place. My trailer was never suitable for him. I was never suitable for him. He wanted me as I retreated, ignored me when I was right in front of him.

I declined the offer, took up more hours at work, and tried to ignore the sound of him sobbing in our bedroom. Though my trailer was dingy, shambled, it was a relief to go back. To lie in bed with nothing but the sound of my cat walking around, the soft sound of my dog breathing. No sound of a heart breaking apart.

MY OWN HEART was a war zone. I felt both freedom and a deep seeded hate for myself. Connor didn't know, yet, that I was talking to Logan. I hated the phrase. Talking to. It was more than that.

"I don't want to have kids." Logan's truth came out on the phone one night. It made my heart bubble up, ache, hiss.

"I don't want them either. Not anymore." He was the first person I'd said it to, before I used it as a weapon on Connor. I sobbed into the phone and he was silent. When I stopped, he shifted, I could hear his clothing rustling.

"Am I the first person you've told that to?"

"Yes. I don't know when I changed my mind. I don't know when it left me, the desire. But I can't tell anyone. Because what would I say? They say I can't let him win. That just because I was touched as a little girl, that doesn't mean I can't be a good mom. But what do they know? I have this hole inside of my chest and there is nothing to fill it. It gets bigger every day and I am drowning. The only way to make the hurt go away is to write. And no one understands that either. We are just sharing to a stupid app on a phone, right? That's what they'll say. It can't fill the hole a child could, but they don't have to live with it. This blackness. This stain."

We were feeling each other out, exploring the possibilities. He lived in Seattle, half a country away.

He sent me pictures of himself by the sea, reading novels I'd never heard of, writing words I wanted tattooed on my skin.

Late at night, he would whisper his desire for me, in English, sometimes in broken French.

I learned, after seeing a screenshot, that after the first night we spoke on the phone, when I belonged to another, he said he was in love with me.

"I'm in love with Gwen," it said.

"In love? Like legit in love?" my friend replied.

"Both? How is this possible? How can you be in love with someone you've never met?" he said.

It scared me to see that. It set me on fire. I told myself it was because he was young. He would change his mind when he met me. The idea of me was so much more enticing than the reality. They always left when they accepted the reality.

I BOUGHT A PLANE TICKET. I flew to Seattle to meet him. But not before giving him the chance to betray me. Not before Connor came to my work in the middle of the day and proposed to me.

PITY, NOT LOVE

Connor

THE FIRST TIME I PROPOSED, it was a desperate act.

I arrived at her work and asked someone at the front counter of the store to tell her I was there. I could see the pity of Gwen's coworkers clearly. They all knew she left me. I thanked the lady and walked into the jewelry department, the racks tall and white.

Gwen found me a couple of minutes later. "Hey," she said, her arms crossed over her chest.

"How are you?" It was a stupid thing to say. I knew how she was. I saw it in the weight she had dropped, I saw it every night when I came home before she moved out. I found a sad comfort in the fact that she hadn't found a nice new place away from me. I hoped she would change her mind and come back, take me back. I hoped she would say yes to me there, then, let me pull her into my arms. I knew my chances were slim. Her eyes were more grey-blue than the vivid color I was used to when she looked at me. I saw pity, not love, when she turned my way.

What's it like to love a man and feel no love in return from him, only to leave him, and feel it all rush back? Was it too late?

"Same as I was last week," she said flatly.

I hovered before she moved out. I walked her to her car and I followed her around the house as she got ready. I hated myself for it. I didn't care if she was in the house before. Then I became desperate for her. I didn't deserve her.

I stepped toward her and she stepped back. I let out a sigh and felt a vise on my heart. Why was I doing this? I was a fucking idiot but I had to try.

"I know you probably hate me right now. And I know you've heard me say all of this before, but I need to say it again. I'm so sorry about everything and I promise you I can change. I can't live without you. Now that you've moved out, I just walk around the house. I feel so lost."

"Go to work. You'll feel better if you get out of the house."

"Do you feel better?"

"Somewhat. Why are you here? I have work to do." She glanced around to see if anyone was watching us.

"I just needed to ask you something." I fumbled in my jacket. The ring box felt heavy, my stomach rolled. I didn't look at her when I dropped to my knees. I fell to both of them. I heard her breath come out, then I looked up at her. The tears were hot and sticky on my face. "I know it's probably too late but I promise you if you say yes, we can make this work. I'll change. I'll pay more attention to you. I'll take you on dates. We will start over."

"Stand up," she said, desperate, looking around again.

"No, I can't until you look at me. Listen to me."

"You've said all of this," her voice broke. I saw tears threatening to fall at the corner. "We are too far gone. I don't feel the same. And how could I tell anyone we were engaged with dignity? You finally propose, after all the years of that being the only thing I wanted, just because I left you? Was I not good enough to marry until I was gone? I can't do that. I deserve better than that. You should have done this years ago."

"I know. I was just waiting for everything to be perfect. I was too stupid to realize it would never be perfect." I had ruined it, deliberately, foolishly.

"I can't accept this proposal. It's not fair to either of us. I don't feel the same and I won't accept it. I won't." I heard the anger boiling at the edges. "I can't believe you came here to do this. Stand up now."

I stood and closed the ring box, staring at the blue carpet. "I'm sorry. I just can't lose you. I can't eat, I can't sleep. I feel like I'm going insane."

"That's how I felt for years. Never good enough for you. Some of that was in my head, some of that was you. I can't keep living like that. You shouldn't have come here, to my work, and done this. Did you really think I would say yes?"

"No. But I had to try. I couldn't live with myself if I didn't." I ran my hand down my face, over my beard. It had started to turn whiter, just as the hair under my ball cap was. I had dropped fifteen pounds in five days. Grief can alter your body rapidly.

Grief had been altering her heart for years and I ignored it.

She was right. She didn't deserve this. And I didn't deserve her.

SILENT MOURNING

"I DIDN'T TELL many people about me and Logan in the beginning. I guarded our relationship fiercely. It seemed absurd, meeting someone thousands of miles away, falling. And I knew it looked bad. Though I was falling further and further for him, I wanted to spare Connor's feelings."

"But he found out eventually, right?"

"Yes. Soon." I think of his frantic texts, his tears. I still can't forgive myself for being so careless.

"What were you doing with your time before you finally met Logan?"

"I was going out more, finding myself in the company of my old friends again. And I found my trailer to be both a refuge and a terrible reminder of the fact that I was getting nowhere in life. I left the fragile walls of that place at twenty-nine, now I was back at thirty-two. Living in a dingy trailer, similar to the ones I grew up in as a child. The sounds of domestic disputes and bonfire parties in the court no longer lulled me to sleep. It was strange what you could find comfort in. Those sounds ringed of my own failure. I missed my two-story house, my quiet street, but it wasn't worth the silence and silent mourning I felt there."

"What made it start to feel like home? Did it ever feel like home again?"

"Connor started to leave plants on my doorstep. He made sure to drop them off early, just before I would leave for work, so the cold wouldn't kill them. He knew I loved to buy green lush plants. It was March and the stores were starting to get them in stock. I was able to open the windows of my trailer. The plants cleansed me, cleansed the air."

"Was it hard to accept those gifts?"

"Yes. I told him to stop, but he wouldn't listen at first. Finally, I told him that every time he left me a gift – and those weren't the only ones, there were flowers being sent to work – I told him it reminded me of what I did to him. And it made me sad, brought no happiness. I told him it was selfish to leave them. He was trying to make me love him again. He didn't care that all I wanted was to be happy again. He just wanted to be happy again."

60

TWO CRASHING CARS

Me: You can break me open. If anyone can, it's you.

Logan: I hope I can. I'm fucking crazy about you.

Me: Why?

Logan: Because you make me feel things I've never experienced.

Me: But why?

Logan: Because of the type of person you are. You're the most genuine person I've ever met. Or, I'm about to meet.

Me: Tell me now. Again. I need to hear it.

Logan: I'm head over heels for you. I've never been so consumed with someone like this. Ever. I dream of you. Good things, not my nightmares. They're gone because of you.

Logan: I'm drinking and I know you're asleep but I needed you to know this.

Logan: I want you. I miss you even though we've never met. I can't wait to kiss you, and I have fallen so fucking hard for you.

OUR TEXTING WAS FOREPLAY, and we both wanted more. We couldn't live without knowing what it would be like to meet in person.

When I saw Logan for the first time he was shorter than I had hoped, but the way he walked was hypnotizing. I hated the shape of my thighs, the wrinkles around my eyes. I had obsessed about every detail on the plane, nearly threw up when I landed.

I was suddenly very aware that I was seven years older than him, but God, the way he smiled as he walked toward me made my thighs ache. I was unhinged, shy.

I covered my face with my hand, listened to the sound of his Converse on the sidewalk outside of the airport. "Oh my god," I said.

He grabbed my hand and pulled me up, wrapped his arms around my entire body, pulled me from the ground.

My arms found their way around his neck. His hair fanned my face and I wanted to cry, but I couldn't let him see it. I felt like I'd known him my entire life and everything had led to this. I wavered on the soulmate debate in the past, but this felt like the nail in the coffin, the nail in my hypothesis.

I heard his voice and it coiled around me. The late-night calls, the video chats, they didn't compare to this.

He was flesh and blood and the most beautiful man I ever laid eyes on, this walking embodiment of everything I wanted, everything I needed. I felt like I had written him into existence. I had been working on my novel for years, and everything I wanted in a man, everything Connor was not giving me, I wrote into a character. I wrote out my desires. This soft voiced man, seven years younger than his love interest. This artist. This broken human. I wrote that character, then I found Logan. The embodiment of everything I thought couldn't be real. It seemed like a dream.

His teeth were not perfect, but there was more in that smile than I could ever write about.

I'd been chasing perfection too maybe, just like Connor, but every man who matched every little check off mark on my list, they were beneath him. I wouldn't recover from this, and I knew it would be something I had to recover from.

He set me on the ground and I saw in his eyes a warming affection, but fireworks were far from blazing. I pushed the idle inspection aside and let him take my carry-on suitcase.

MY FRIENDS and I dissected everything about what the first meeting would be like. They said he would take me into his arms, kiss me immediately. I said he wouldn't. My gut told me we would be too shy. I was right. I'd been in his presence for an hour and I knew I couldn't go any longer.

We were lying on his bed, on our sides, facing each other.

His room was a mess. The same kind of frat room I'd been avoiding for so many years, but his age made me forgive it, and he had just moved in.

I ran my fingers over his forearm, over the fresh ink on his arm.

"God," he said. "I feel like I've been waiting forever for this. For you to touch me."

"Sit back," I said. He pulled himself up, leaned his back against the wall. I crawled across the bed and straddled him, but I did not kiss him.

I felt in control and it was thrilling. It was the thing I always craved, the control I could normally only find with younger men.

I grazed my lips over the vein in his neck and I felt him shiver.

It was too much. How could I keep my lips from him when he sighed like that? I wanted to play the game but he won with that vulnerable sigh. I thought then, that maybe, the games would be done, finally.

This kiss, it would go down as one of the single most perfect moments of my life. He and I could not overcome what was between us. Thirty-two and twenty-five, half a country apart.

I told myself he would be in my life for just a moment because a burning like this couldn't be real.

He would be in my life for just one moment to wreck it. To show me what belief was. The cynic in me could not compete with the cynic in him.

We were too alike. The same scars, the same mental ticking, ready to implode. Every experiment needs a control group, and we were two crashing cars. I needed someone to steady me. He needed someone to steady him.

We would be a slow-burning fire, a spark that died quickly, leaving scars. I had three more days with him and I would make sure I was touching him for every moment of those days and hours.

How can you say hello and goodbye to someone all at once, with one kiss? We had shared so much, so many virtual confessions. I wanted to confess to him with my skin for as long as I could. Before my plane took off.

I didn't believe him when he said I was safe with him. He meant it, but it was a lie. Maybe he knew it, maybe he didn't, but I determined right there and then that I would give him almost every bit of my heart. I would save the smallest, most vulnerable bit. Because I did not trust him with it.

This boy had more power in his lips than others had in their entire body to wound me.

I'd rather be wounded by a man who meant to, than by a man who thought he was there to save me. Who convinced himself he was whole enough to save a drowning woman. He could never love me the way the man I had just broken could. He was too broken himself.

61

A COWARD AND A LIAR

"I OFTEN FOUND myself so set on a revenge, of sorts. When a man did me wrong, I abandoned all loyalty to him. The high of Logan didn't last long. When I got back home to Missouri, I learned he wronged me before I even had a chance to see him face-to-face. His ex-girlfriend, someone he couldn't let go of yet, had flown out to see him two weeks before I did. I silently said a prayer that I found out after my trip. The plane ticket was bought, paid for. I did not check the trip insurance box. I was going whether I wanted to or not. We didn't speak of the wrong he did after that one phone call two days after I got home. I buried it, the way I always did. A flicker of Connor flashed across my mind when the truth hit."

"Why did he come to mind?"

"He wouldn't have pulled that shit with me. Well, maybe six or seven years ago he would have. But we were long past that. His weapons had become his walls. Not deceit. Not another girl. When I landed back in Missouri, I pushed Logan from my mind for a few days. I didn't text him in the twenty-four hours after I got home. I left my phone home on purpose. When I got home from work, I found a dozen frantic texts and five missed calls from him. Wondering what was wrong. Why I was ignoring him. I thought about the tables and if they had been turned. If a guy had flown across the country to see me and then ghosted me when he got home. I wanted to feel guilty, but I had it in my gut. The knowledge that he was a temporary part of my life.

"And the saddest part of it all, was that I knew, deep in my gut, that I loved him. I loved him in a way that was completely separate from my love for Connor. From anything I felt for him. They existed in different realms of my heart. That little barren wasteland somehow had enough space for my love of two men. It had been ripping me apart for the entire year. It was only April and I knew I couldn't survive the rest of the calendar days like that. Split in two. Denying both men my wholeness. Connor's frantic texts stopped a week after I landed, after my layover call with him, after he saw the picture I uploaded to my Instagram of Logan and me on the beach."

"That's how he learned about Logan?"

"Yes. I was a coward and a liar. He knew then, that my loneliness wasn't the only reason I left him. I wanted to drown in a black hole. My empty bedroom with no thoughts of love or longing. No thoughts of what I was turning into. I thought of Connor's family. I could never go back. They knew who I was. The damage I had done. I imagined him telling them. Telling them it wasn't just that he drove me away. The truth was I fell for another man. I wish he hadn't let me. I wish he had held onto my whole heart." I let tears warm my cheeks, thinking of who I became three years ago. "His distance had let me turn into the one thing I hated most. The two-faced villain. The same kind of sinner my ex-lovers had been. Did I turn Avery to this kind of sin? Did he feel lonely with me?" I think of his skin under mine when he cheated on Wendy. "No. I was not him." Men cheated to feel fresh flesh. Women cheated to ease the ache of a loneliness they tried to wish away.

"But you mended things with Logan, right?"

"A Band-Aid forgiveness, the kind I was good at. After a few days, I started to warm to Logan again. But I was changed. I no longer let romance into my language. No hope of a future. Just a *here and now* mentality. And I felt it in him, too. He would later tell me he never wanted us to not know each other. In those words, I felt the fluttering of what I feared most. His blackout from my life. He said it because he felt it, too. That one day, we wouldn't know each other."

I look down at my hands, my shaking hands. "We savored the days. Every night at 2 a.m. I woke to his texts. Telling me about his day, calling me sometimes. I lost more weight and the bags under my eyes grew to large pools. Losing sleep for him was a drug, and I didn't care. My life was sepia and my tongue was that of a serpent. A month later, Connor called. I answered. He didn't bring Logan up. He didn't bring up the way I ruined him. He talked to me like a friend and I wondered if he was seeing someone. If someone was sleeping in the bed we bought in the house I decorated. Parking in my spot in the driveway."

"Would you have been jealous if you knew there was someone there?"

"I was filled with a mixture of emotions that moved through me fluidly. Jealousy over a phantom. Thankfulness over a phantom. I wanted his happiness but a tiny little voice inside wanted to rip it away, if he had it. I wanted to be the only one who gave it to him. He asked me out to dinner. I said no. He asked me to go for a walk with him. So I said yes. It seemed harmless. I loved our old neighborhood. I felt safe there. The old trailer park was depressing me. I would ask myself every night, as I tried to sleep after seeing Logan's name light up my phone, how I got back there. Maybe Connor knew I would want that warmth again. I loved the colors of the row houses. The shutters. My old mailbox was blue and I always felt blue when I looked at it. When I saw it again, I thought of the day Connor painted it. He said he wanted it to match the color of my eyes. I wondered if he kept the keys on the walls. All the ones I collected while we were together. I should have taken them with me but the walls of the trailer were better bare, better with boxes stacked against them. A past I didn't want to reopen."

"Why did you still talk to Logan every night?"

"He understood things Connor never could."

"What kind of things?"

"Abuse, neglect." I hesitate. Do I have a right to tell Logan's story? What was done to him? How he saw a therapist as a child. Then a psychologist. Is it my right to tell anyone about the medication he had to take, to battle the night terrors? The images of a woman entering his room, taking his heart in her red hands? "When I graduated high school, my father didn't show. It had been three years since he and my mother had split, and his presence had been scarce when they were together as it was. Being let down by him was the norm. I was used to it, used to the pit in my stomach when waiting for him. For phone calls, for birthday presents, for any type of attention. So his absence was expected. What wasn't expected, was the cost. A cost Logan understood."

"What was the cost?"

"My hair began to fall out in clumps over the summer. It was a strange cocktail, that year. My father was a no-show. My high school boyfriend, the guy I had lost my virginity to, cheated on me five days after I gave it up. I was living at home still, which was no surprise. I had no plan for after school. I had no interest in college and the thought of being out in the world frightened me. I developed an unhealthy dependence on the shitty boyfriend who betrayed me. Instead of kicking him to the curb, I took him back. Forgiveness is not always the answer. It's a weakness. One I own, fully."

"That's why you think you forgave Logan? Because you're weak?"

"Yes. Because he was the only one I had ever been able to talk to about my family. He didn't pity me. He understood me. He knew what it felt like to want to take your life, but his thoughts hadn't been idle, like mine. When he was a teen, he tried. And I'm so thankful he failed. After living with a man for years who would show me nothing of his heart, I clung to Logan. I would take him any way I could. I would take his friendship if it was all we could share."

62

HEART IN A GLASS JAR

LOGAN'S AN ARTIST. He writes poetry. He paints. He helped his father build the house he lived in as a teenager to escape the pain his aunt caused him, the same kind my father caused me. He loves to sing in the shower, in the kitchen, in bed. When I visited him on the coast we wrote together in silence, then shared our poems. We walked along the beach at night. We took tequila shots and laughed. He always calls me by my full name. He's a wonderful uncle, a passionate friend. He made love to me like I wasn't something delicate, like I wouldn't break. Because he knew how resilient humans could be, he knew we could come back from what was stolen from us.

He had no desire to have children. He reminds me that I am still a woman, even though I no longer want to bring life into this world. The innocence we lost, bloomed bright between our palms when he reached for me for the first time.

His voice is soft, nearly as soft as his hands.

Still, I won't let my guard down. He lied and I cannot forget that. I don't care that the girl visited him before me, not after.

My mother had told me to always be the one who loved less. I failed before, and recovering was still something I was unable to do. I will always keep my heart in a glass jar. No one, no one but myself, is allowed to break me. No one can have that kind of control over me.

WHEN CONNOR CAME to my work four weeks after finding out about me and Logan, I pulled him down an aisle, leveled him with my eyes. "What are you doing here?"

"I need new dishes; you took ours." He didn't frown or say it in a tone that sounded defensive. There was humor in his voice. He wanted me to see his heart wasn't broken. That he was moving on. Buying new dishes with the help of the ex who took his. I wanted to shove him and make him go away.

He looked good. Slim and tan. The sallow color of his skin was gone. The hollow look in his eyes was gone, too.

"Are you going to help me pick some?"

I think my mouth fell open a little. He laughed and walked away, calling over his shoulder, "Come on, heartbreaker, you owe me."

I followed him, recalling the way I followed him, for years, blindly.

We made it to the housewares section. His hands were on his hips; he had shorts on and I thought he knew what he was doing. His legs were always one of the things I loved the most about him. The years of hockey had been kind to him. The fabric was pulled taut over his ass, also made of marble. What an ass. No, more like what an asshole.

"So, what do you want?" I crossed my arms, pretended to stare at the dishes surrounding us, but I was really looking to make sure none of my coworkers were witnessing this.

"I want you, but that's not going to happen," he said, then quickly talked again, not letting me reply. "I think this pattern looks nice."

He pointed to a black and white china pattern. It was the opposite of the dishes I had taken with me. If I moved back in, by some strange turn of events, they wouldn't match at all.

I walked away and came back with a plate. I held it in the air and he nodded, so I turned and he followed me to the display in the corner.

I started to gather them and Connor helped, grazing his fingers along mine as he went. I glared at him and he just laughed, not even trying to hide what he was doing.

We hadn't touched in so long. My skin was on fire. I thought of Logan. Of the last time we talked.

I saw a coworker walk by, eyes wide, recognizing my ex. I rolled my eyes and shrugged my shoulders. I didn't know what the fuck I was doing here. I should have let one of the other girls help him.

I fell right into his trap. I felt like I was in a time warp, back to five or six years ago, when he had me wrapped around his little finger.

"Would you like to come over sometime? Help me break in my new dinnerware?"

"Is that why you came here? You could get dishes anywhere, you know."

"Oh for sure, I'm here to see you. To show you how great I look, to tell you how great you look. I haven't given up on us and I doubt I ever will. It's you for me, that's it."

I stared at him, blinked, and started eyeing the dishes again.

"I know you can't see it yet, but we are supposed to be together. After everything we have been through, how could we not be?" He ran his hand over the edge of a mug, inspecting it.

"We didn't work out though."

"Yeah, we didn't. But I see it now. We needed this. I was a shitty boyfriend. I've never been so lost." His eyes went dark. "I didn't know I was the kind of guy who would cry that much. I've fallen apart in front of my sister, my mother, my father, the owner of the gym, and trust me, that was a low moment. But I'm not embarrassed. I don't care. I don't know why I let myself be that man before. The kind who doesn't feel. I feel everything now. You've done that to me, for me. And now, I'm doing this for you."

"Doing what?" I tried not to roll my eyes.

"Showing you what it's like to have someone love you no matter what. No matter how much they hurt you. This love I have for you, it's unconditional."

We gathered dishes in silence. I tried to figure out what to say next. I couldn't reply. I had no words for him. What was unconditional love? It was a death trap. It made you stupid.

"I really think I want to move," I said, reaching for a white plate with black edging. I pulled eight pieces from the rack and walked to a nearby register, starting a stack.

"Where to?" Connor reached for a bowl, turned it over.

"The Pacific Northwest."

"Really? Is this something new? Or have you always wanted to live there?" There was an unspoken question there. He didn't know what beach I had been on when he saw the picture of me and Logan. He was figuring it out.

"New I guess. I just want to get out of here." A hint. A little barb. He needed to stop looking at me like that. He was brushing up against me too, as he carried dishes to his pile. It had been so long since he flirted with me. I wasn't sure what to make of it.

"I understand. Sometimes, I want to leave, too. I love my family. But it was nice being away from the Midwest during college. I could move again."

"You could?" I thought of his family, of the way he talked about them, the way he loved them. They were just words. He couldn't leave them. And I couldn't understand that. I could leave my family, my home, in a heartbeat.

"Yeah. If you wanted to go, I could go, too." His words were warm, safe. I recoiled, then recovered.

"I'm not asking you to move with me. Or for me." I'd never wanted someone to give anything up for me. I never wanted to be a regret.

"I know that. I'm just telling you that I would. I would, if you wanted that."

"This is a dumb conversation. We need to stop." I went to walk away but Connor raised his hands in the air. The overhead light above him reflected his new grey hairs.

"I'm sorry. I don't know why I said that. It's just, when I see you it's hard to not think of you as my girlfriend. It just came out."

I didn't believe him. He was being deliberate. He was trying to plant seeds. "Okay. Let's finish this set." I grabbed a wide rimmed bowl. "This is nice."

"But do you like them?" He raised an eyebrow, his dark eyes so large and beautiful.

"They're nice."

"Okay, good. I want something you'd like."

I helped him pick his new dishes, and he left. I watched him go.

THAT NIGHT I matched with a younger guy on Tinder and invited him over when the weekend rolled around. His new face and new hands on my body erased, for a night, the stains Logan and Connor were leaving on me.

63

SPENT OF SALT

IT WAS a Tuesday night when I got the call. My mother was crying. She told me my stepfather was dead. That he had been dead for months. The funeral had passed and no one even told my brother. I knew why no one told me. We had been estranged for a while. But in his stubbornness, he had let his own son go without a chance to tell him goodbye. I had never known a man with more hate and ugliness in his heart.

I fell to my front steps after I hung up. I clutched my chest and I wept. Then I threw up in the rose bush under my window. No one tells you how it'll feel, to mourn a monster. To still feel the well of tears and the wave of fire under your skin. The warring elation and the memories you stored deep in your chest, the good ones. The mourning of those of that person you built up, convinced yourself had a little bit of goodness still in them.

I thought about skinned knees and learning to ride my bike. I thought of my tiny hand in his as we crossed the street. I thought of the silver jewelry case he bought me and the time I ran away from home, trying to get to his house, when I was fighting with my mother after they split.

My mind had saved me then. It kept from me the truth of his violent hands and his terrible, disgusting heart in his chest. I wept for my mother, who didn't know she was crying for the man who had broken me. The same way she had been broken by a man.

So many sick patterns were being repeated.

I needed to call my brother. Find out how he was doing. I wouldn't be upset with him if he was upset, even though he knew what was done to me. I had worked up the courage to tell him finally. And yes, if he was sad over this death, I would understand it. I would understand that there are things in life we cannot understand.

I called Logan when I made it inside. There was no answer. I stripped my clothes and ran a bath. It was there, that the floodgates opened. I was not spent of salt. There was more to come.

I watched my phone from the corner of my eye, it never lit up.

I didn't know who else to tell. They wouldn't understand, wouldn't know what to say. They would say they were sorry. I had lost my stepfather, they didn't know the complexities of it all.

I was sitting on my bed staring at the wall with my pen in my hand when Connor called. I answered, brought the phone to my face. A lifeless "hello" fell into the air.

"What's wrong? Are you okay? I felt like I needed to call you."

"How did you know?"

"I don't know. It's weird. I could feel you."

"Come over," I said, then hung up.

MY DEPRESSION GOT WORSE over the summer. My stepfather was finally dead and I punished myself when that brought me relief. I wrote more. When I wasn't in my room, in bed, I was out drinking with Kate. She had moved back from Tennessee.

I bounced around between barely sleeping and sleeping away my days off.

Logan and I slipped into a friendship that I wrote into the grave. He spoke in vague wantings. He never brought up the option of me visiting again.

I had a work trip planned for Seattle in August and we pretended it was a ghost.

I didn't tell him that Connor came to comfort me when he didn't answer my phone calls about my stepfather's death. I just let him comfort me the next day over the phone. I pretended I had been waiting for it. That he was the only one who would understand. It was a partial truth. Connor couldn't understand the way Logan could, but he was there. He felt my pain and picked up the phone. He showed up, for once.

He was different, open and pouring his feelings at my feet, where once he was nothing but a tall wall.

It was unsettling, choking. Again I reached for a new face, something to get me away from the pull and push of my love for two flawed men. One I couldn't have, one I wouldn't let myself have.

IN SOME WAY

TWO WEEKS later Connor picked me up in his Range Rover and took me to the car wash where my car had died. The drive was slow, a torture I deserved. I thought of my last phone call with Logan. It was such a silly thing, to get so caught up in him. My theory was wrong. Younger men could hurt me the same way men my age could.

I was staring out the window when Connor spoke. He asked me what was wrong and I didn't speak. I kept my head away. My throat was on fire and I couldn't let the man whose heart I had broken see me falling apart over the man I left him for.

"It's nothing," I said, finally. The inside of his vehicle was stifling.

"I know you probably think I want to see you sad. But I don't. I don't want you with that guy, but I don't want to see you hurting. Is it your stepdad? Is that it?"

"No." I wouldn't forget the way Connor hugged me on my steps. It was the reason I was with him now; I had started to need him again. "And *he* and I aren't together, we never were. Besides, I can't talk to you about that."

But who could I talk to? I was numbing myself. I was drinking a lot.

Kate and I would go out on the weekends, weeknights, day drinking.

"You need to eat too," she would say.

"I know." *I knew I knew I knew.* But no one could know the ache of my body, the pressure in between my ears. I had found a likeness, someone as broken as I, and the drifting was all at once, all-encompassing.

"Why not?" Connor said, beside me. "Why can't you talk about him to me?"

I received little gifts in the mail, from time to time, from Logan. Books he had read, handwritten notes, dusted with sand, that he had written before surfing.

This past Tuesday, I saw an oversized envelope in my mailbox after work. They always brought a smile to my face. I never knew when one was coming, what it would bring. And I needed a smile, after everything with my stepfather. I liked that about Logan, that even though we talked on the phone, and texted, he liked to send me letters and gifts. I wondered if he had sent it specifically to cheer me up.

I was wrong. That day would bring a gift that was an omen I could not deny, one I would feel the echo of, for weeks, years.

I walked into my trailer, throwing my purse on the floor as I turned the package over. I ripped at the envelope as I called for Holly.

I fed my dog and sat down at my kitchen table. Logan sent me a copy of Go Ask Alice. Inside was a note, telling me why he thought I should read it.

I sent him a text and flipped through the worn paperback. My phone buzzed on the table, pulling my eyes from the dark cover.

Logan: I'm glad you got the book.
Logan: And I want you to know, I think you're pretty amazing.
Me: I'm so glad I know you.

Logan had brought out a part of me I didn't know existed. A hopeful heart, pulling healing from somewhere deep. I felt him drifting, and then moments like this brought back the blooming, the memories. Of nights spent on the phone with him. Confessions, and judgment never passed. My cheeks were warm as I flipped through the pages of the book again. My phone buzzed in my hand again.

Logan: I'm glad I know you, too. And I hope we always do know each other, in some way.

I stared at the screen. *In some way. In some way. In some way.* No. My gut clenched. I walked to my bathroom, in a trance. My hand moved on its own, turning the bathroom faucet on. I took a bath in steaming water. My flesh was red and blotchy when I got out.

When I made it back to my bed, I found my phone, clicked the side button, lighting it up. I saw another text from Logan.

Logan: Hey, you how that poet Mary? She is in town for work and she is going to come hang with me and the guys tonight. She knows you. She said she loves your work, and to say hello.

I didn't respond. I didn't sleep.

The next morning, I woke, from my fitful napping, to a text from Logan at 2 a.m. He wanted to know what I was doing.

It should have quelled the nagging, the dreaded anvil, the knowing animal eating me alive. He had been drifting slowly, he was like the waves. And a text at 2 a.m. meant he was thinking of me, right? And I shouldn't worry? I couldn't convince myself of that.

Over the next weeks, he would pull further and further away.

One's intuition should never be ignored. I knew what happened. I knew it, and I pushed it down, let it become a seed.

And I became the wall I told him I would never be with him. No, I wouldn't talk to Connor about this. "It's weird," I said, pushing the melancholy away.

"It's only weird if you think it is. I want to be your friend."

"You can't be in a relationship with someone for five years and then suddenly be friends just months after you split up, or ever."

"What rule book did you read that in? You've always done this. Said what we can or cannot do. You put that in your own head. You let other people convince you of that."

"You'll just be happy about anything I tell you. You won't be able to help it. And I'm not going to share any of it with you. Or anything." Maybe I should have offered him that kindness, the when and why of my heartbreak over Logan. He deserved to know he was right, that he had gotten what he hoped for.

"Well, I'm here if you want to talk. Just always know that."

"We couldn't talk when we were together." I turned to him.

"Well, I'm a different person. I don't know how to explain it." He put his vehicle in park, next to mine, broken down and dirty. It was a good thing we were at the car wash.

I didn't hear a lie in Connor's voice. He genuinely didn't want to see me sad. I wish he had been more concerned about my mental well-being when we were together. Hindsight and all that.

Maybe he would be a better partner for the next woman he ended up in a relationship with. I couldn't entertain the idea of us getting back together. I couldn't face his family, his friends, after what I had done.

"I've been listening to some great music," he said, changing the subject.

I finally looked ahead. My cheeks no longer tear stained. "Oh yeah?"

"I found this guy, Jason Isbell. I love him. I'll send you some songs."

"Okay," I replied, not really wanting to look for hidden meaning in the songs he had been listening to alone in our home.

His therapy was music, mine was writing. I had recently landed an agent, a publishing deal. Things were looking up in my writing career. One I never thought I would have. It was the beginning of a life I had always dreamed about but never thought would become a reality.

Maybe one day I would escape. That's all I thought about. I was always wanting to escape to somewhere other than where I was.

EASY AND DEVASTATING

"WHAT IS SEX TO YOU? Fun? Necessary? Is it the escape you say you're always looking for?"

"It's a weapon," I say. I pull my drink to my lips and sip. "I took what was used against me and made it my own. I use it. I've used it. It's easy and devastating."

"You seek to crave control above all else. And the younger men are an extension of that."

"Yes. It took me years to figure out why I craved younger men. And it took one man to make me realize that younger men can break you the same way older men can. I just needed men in my bed that were as far removed from the image of my stepfather as I could manage. Toward the end of my relationship with Connor we barely touched each other, barely had sex. I had slipped into an existence that had no intimacy, no touch in it. So when I was free, I wanted to kiss as many beautiful men as I could. Convince myself I was invincible, that I couldn't be touched."

"But you were spending time with Connor again, right?"

"Yes. We would walk our dogs. I had taken mine and he kept his dog. We told each other, ourselves, that it was so we could make them happy." I laugh, thinking of when Connor would tell me what a good mother I would be, if I just let myself try. That my love for animals convinced him of it.

"I didn't tell Logan I was spending time with Connor. Connor knew I was still talking to Logan, but he knew it was falling apart, and he didn't care to steal me from that. That was our way. When we were apart, we never cared to steal each other. When we wanted each other, nothing could stand in our way. But I didn't want him again, not yet. I wanted to play more. To lick my wounds. To pretend Logan and I would see each other in Seattle and it wouldn't hurt."

EASY TO ROMANTICIZE

I LIKED his voice and the way he looked at me with his brown eyes. From the stage, his guitarist yelled my way, "Hey, red pants!"

I had worn them to be seen, by the singer, by the crowd, by anyone who would drown my emptiness.

Connor texted me "Have fun down there" as I crossed the border out of Missouri with Kate. We were becoming friends, it was strange and he made me laugh. I didn't know what to do with it. I should have been staying away from him, letting him move on. I wanted to feel guilty about the time spent with him and my trip down south, but we weren't together anymore. I shouldn't have been spending time with him again, but I missed him.

Five years together and I didn't know how to get on without him like I thought.

I knew how to do the simple things; get to work, make shitty TV dinners, fuck. That was about it.

There was a helplessness I felt without him, and an unhinged mania.

It was intoxicating. I wanted to run my train off the tracks. I wanted to hurt myself, to get in a bind so bad that someone would force me to face these demons.

One demon stared at me from the stage. He was tall, 6'2", with a voice that should be on the radio. I'd never touched him but I knew that night I would. We'd started talking online, and we'd already agreed to it.

Two artists under city lights. I told myself maybe I could survive, be happy, with an artist. Connor always wanted to be practical.

I just wanted to write, to see where it led. It got me here, to Wade. I went to the bar and ordered a cape-codder.

When the bartender handed it to me I took a sip. It was all cranberry. I tasted no vodka. I asked her if she would make it stronger and Kate narrowed her eyes at me. She knew what I was doing. I just didn't want to pay for a downtown Nashville drink and be stiffed.

When she came back, she handed me a shot of vodka to put into the drink. I downed it instead and shivered as my phone vibrated in my pocket.

I saw Kate glance at the singer and back to me. I wouldn't look his way again, not yet. I looked at my phone and saw Logan's name on it. I cursed him and showed Kate my phone.

"Don't talk to him. No wait, I'm texting him." I let her. It didn't matter. *No, loving artists wasn't the answer.*

Fucking one probably wasn't either, but what could it hurt? I was already too damaged, too broken up. My safe place awaited me back in Missouri. But I was not ready.

I was not riddled with enough scares. I swiveled in my seat and watched Wade sing. He didn't look my way and I felt the challenge. I needed him to acknowledge me. I needed the reminder that he wanted me. His voice made my skin flush.

When the set ended, Wade left the bar and I felt a bubble of rage take over me. I broke my shoes in the streets and Kate bought me a new pair. I was about to drive away in an Uber when Wade told me to come to my favorite bar in Nashville. I was standing outside of it, wondering how he got in. Then I remembered he played there. He probably came in through the back.

I ADDED him to my list. When I sobered up, later that night, after he fed me water for an hour, I took his clothes off in his downtown apartment. I forgot Logan and I forget Connor and I pretended I had new skin. I stole Wade's shirt the next morning and I never saw him again. I wrote poems about him just because he was easy to romanticize, but you can't build a life off of men like that. You can build one off of men who see all your shattered pieces, who let you break them, but still want you.

Connor wanted me. I didn't know why, after everything I did. After Logan, and my leaving. I could never forgive someone for that. I forgave Connor for so much so many years ago, but now I was the villain again.

We were always switching hats. I wanted a balance. I wanted us to love each other at the same time. To have the same fire, the same passion.

There was a numbness in me now that I wasn't sure would ever fade away.

I thought when my stepfather died, it would go away, but all summer I had been burning bridges, hurting myself.

How can you explain away the feeling of sadness you have when your stepfather, the only father you've ever known, dies? When it's the same stepfather who molested you? There is a hate there, a self-hate, that cannot be washed away. I once wanted children, and he stole that from me. I felt like a broken car on the side of the road. He was the freeway, stretching out into oblivion.

PAST REPEATING ITSELF

"The first time I felt jealousy again, I was dropping something off for Connor. I was back in my old neighborhood, so I stopped in with one of his old ball caps. It was stuck in with my summer clothes. When I saw the car parked on the street in front of my old house I felt my face blaze, but I lied to myself, I told myself it had to belong to someone across the street. When Connor answered the door, my old door, he was shirtless and sleepy eyed. I gave him his ball cap and left quickly, not hearing what he was calling after me."

"Who was it?"

I smile, because now, she is no threat to my heart. "A married woman. An ex."

"Sounds like the past repeating itself."

"Yes, different weapons, different hands. I couldn't blame him. I was stringing him along, going for walks with him. Holding his hand when he reached for it. I never let myself kiss him. I never let myself sleep with him. I worried I would just slip back into my old life, and I wasn't ready for it. I still had goodbyes to say."

68

BAD PENNY

I DON'T KNOW why I said yes. Having dinner at Connor's house would be considered a bad idea, to any other person but me. But I was curious. I wanted to know what my house looked like. I wanted to see if a woman had been inside. If the car I had seen after I returned from Nashville was a figment of my imagination.

WHEN I SHOWED up he walked out of my old gate, to my car door. He opened it and smiled. I saw everything my friends had talked about. His waist was even more narrow, his shoulders more swollen than the last time I saw him. He had a sheen of sweat on his brow.

"What have you been doing?" I glanced over his shoulder, through the open gate, into my old backyard.

"Grilling. Do kabobs sound okay?" His voice was so casual, like we were friends now, or still together. Not a mess of two exes taking walks, holding hands, sleeping with other people. Or, at least I was anyway. I needed to find out if he was.

"Yeah, that's fine." I followed him into my old yard. His dog, our dog, ran up to me and I crouched down to pet him.

"I'll grab you a drink. Head on out back to the deck."

I stood up and walked through the yard, taking in the scenery. He had planted new plants. I peeked into the window that led to the backyard. I was greeted by more greenery. Potted plants. So he was buying them for himself too this past spring.

I always killed them, but I couldn't stop buying them when I lived here. I wanted to start over every spring. I had this hope I could keep something alive.

I had been sitting in the backyard for just a moment when Connor came back, a glass of red, pinkish liquid in his hand.

"What's that?" I pointed to the glass and watched him set it in front of me on the patio table.

"Cape-codder."

I reached forward and took the glass. "I hope you don't care, Kate is coming by to join us." I needed a crutch. He knew it.

"Afraid to be alone with me?" He smiled and walked to the grill.

"Maybe," I said to his back, now facing me. It was going to be so damn awkward. I could tell already.

When Kate showed up, I was half lit. She gave me a knowing smirk and maybe rolled her eyes. I couldn't tell. We settled into the same kind of easy banter we always enjoyed. Connor made fun of Kate. I played referee.

LATER, the conversation entered into dangerous territory. "It's not like you have both been celibate since you broke up," Kate mocked. She knew what I had been up to, and I felt bad. From what I heard, Connor hadn't been out at all. He had been staying home, or at the gym. Working odd and long hours. There was still the mystery of the car though. Maybe he could shed some light on that.

Connor wore a smirk when I met his eyes.

My face went red. No blush, just anger. "Who have you slept with?"

I narrowed my eyes. I didn't have a right to know. I had slept with someone new, more than one someone new. He knew it. Everyone knew it. I felt a sick sadness. A betrayal that I had no right to own. He swore he loved me and now I was learning he had slept with someone new? "What's her name?" I asked. I could see Kate squirm in her seat.

"Doesn't matter." Connor was still smiling, swirling his Jack and Coke.

"Is it someone I know?" Who did I know that Connor would go out and find?

"Yes. It is."

I racked my brain. Connor never looked at other women while we were together. His eyes were only for me, even through the years we barely spoke. I didn't expect him to continue to only look my way after I left him, but maybe some part of me hoped he had. I wanted him to wait for me but I couldn't promise I would come back. I was transported back in time. To the year we met. I always wanted what I couldn't have. Had he moved on? Was this a dinner to tell me he was dating someone new?

"Are you with her? This girl?"

"No. I only want you. You know that." His smile was gone, his dark eyes were almost black.

"But you've been with someone else. Doesn't sound like it." I had some nerve, giving him shit for sleeping with someone after all that I had done. But I wasn't the one claiming to still be in love. I told him I had fallen out of love with him when I left. The vodka made me spiteful. I thought of the last time I had vodka, Wade and his hands, his musical voice. I had thrown away the shirt I stole when I got back to Missouri.

"I needed someone to distract me. I only want you and I've been going about this the wrong way. I should have remembered who you are. I want you to be jealous. Are you jealous?"

Kate stood up. "Okay, I should go. This is very, very awkward for me."

I waved at her, distracted, my only thought on who Connor slept with. "Do I know her? Tell me that."

"Yes, I said that." He laughed. He always made fun of me for repeating myself when I was drunk.

I pulled out my phone and tapped on the Facebook app. I didn't know what I was looking for. Maybe a face would catch my eye, jog my memory. Connor didn't have Facebook. If it was someone I knew, maybe I was friends with her. A name popped into my head. A bad name. A bad penny. I grabbed the drink in front of me and downed it. "You've got to be kidding me." I said it out loud, not to Connor maybe, just to get the words out.

"What?"

"Penny? Why does she always have to put her hands on what I have? And isn't she married?"

"Yes, she is. They are splitting up." He stirred his drink again, and we simmered in the silence. "And you don't have me. You gave me away, for him."

He didn't seem mad when he said it. More amused, knowing he had me. I'd fallen right into his trap. I couldn't believe it. "Was it in our bed?"

"Yes."

I felt a warmth move through me, a slow rolling of rage and possession. It was my house. He was mine. That bed was mine, we bought it together. He was mine. She wouldn't have him. No.

I FUCKED CONNOR THAT NIGHT, on the patio table, inside on the deep-freezer, in our old bed. I wish I could say we made love, we fell back together, but that would be a lie. The truth was that I didn't want another woman touching him. I didn't want another woman pulling him from me. I didn't want to lose him. I realized it that night, but I wasn't ready for him to know.

ANYTHING

Connor

MY PRIDE USED to be something I guarded. I no longer cared about it. I had been ripped open and stretched thin. The past few months had been the most trying of my life.

I took after my mother physically. She had a full head of grey hair, pepper and white, and it was beautiful. My 31st birthday was fast approaching and more grey had grown in since Gwen left me than any other year of my life. Losing her was a blow like no other.

Now, possibly, hopefully, I nearly had her back. And I didn't feel more at ease.

Well, sometimes I did. On the nights she came to my place, her old home, I slept well.

Ever since the night I invited her over for a BBQ she had been spending more time with me. I know her. I've known her for years and I know what it takes to get her desire. I didn't see it at first.

I thought if I told her how much I loved her, how sorry I was, she would come back. Getting through to her with honest words and confessions was useless. She only wanted what she couldn't have.

That's how Gwen operated. She wanted to compete, to win. I had to let her, for a moment, believe she could lose me to another. I knew she would want me again if she knew I was moving on, or thought I was. So I tricked her. I didn't care that it was silly. Anything to have her back. That's what I would do. Anything.

I wanted to propose again. To hear her tell me she loved me the way I loved her. To know she wanted a life with me. To know she was serious about us again. That it wasn't just passing time, what we were doing.

Those years we spent drifting apart, I didn't want to repeat them.

I wanted to show her I was a new man, a new lover, her partner.

She said I didn't try hard enough to get over her. And I agreed because I never wanted to. Not really. I distracted myself. I went through the motions. I just tried to survive, but I needed more.

FOOLISH

"DID FINDING out Connor had slept with another woman bring you back to him?"

"It pulled me to him. And I started to feel like we could try again. We started to spend more time together after that night. It reminded me of years ago, I would go over late at night, except now it was he who wanted more. I was unsure, like he had been before we got together. It was a dance, you know? And I felt like I had a goodbye to take care of."

"Logan?" His name. His beautiful name.

"Yes. I was still in love with him. I knew we would never be together, deep in my gut, but I wanted to see him one last time. I wanted to see him when I flew to Seattle and I couldn't give my heart back to Connor until I closed that door." I was so sure I could make my heart obey my rules back then. So foolish.

"Were you able to close that door when you saw him again?" She knows the answer but she wants me to say it.

"No. It wasn't even closed when I said my vows to Connor the next year."

71

I LOVE YOU, I LOVE YOU

I HAD one free day during my work trip to Seattle. Joe and I were like strangers, we wouldn't be sleeping together, or even hanging out while out of town together. We barely spoke on the plane. It really hammered home that we had nothing in common, and years ago the only thing that brought us together was our physical attraction to each other.

Before I left I texted Logan, telling him an approximate time I would be in my hotel room. I had been up front with him. I told him that soon, I would be off the market.

He didn't ask questions. He had no right to. He knew how I felt and his silence said everything.

Once, over the summer, after downing a few drinks I came close to telling him. Instead, I asked him a question.

"Do you know how I feel about you?" I asked. *I love you, I love you.*

"Yes. Yes I do."

The sound of the waves reached through his phone to me. I wondered about other girls' bare feet, if they left with sand in their shoes, after walking along the coast with him. We never spoke of it again. I wasn't the begging kind.

In Seattle, I made it to my room early, my phone buzzed in my hand as I inserted my keycard with the other.

I walked into my room, threw my purse on the bed, and rolled my suitcase to the chaise lounge in the corner. The screen of my phone made my face warm and crimson when I looked at it.

Logan: I'm downstairs. I couldn't wait.

WHEN I OPENED THE DOOR, I bit my lip and cursed myself for the cliché. I couldn't help it. He had a backpack slung over his shoulder, no suitcase. We only had this day and it was a thorn, a blister. He walked in and dropped his bag, gathering me into his arms. I was lost in the scent of his hair, it was longer, the four months since I last saw him felt tangible.

I wanted to cry, but we had become this tragedy, this walking reminder that love is not enough, especially when only one was in love.

I let go, grabbing his hand, pulling him to the bed.

"How was your flight?"

"Horrible. I barely slept." We had arrived at the airport at 4 a.m. I hadn't slept the night before, I couldn't stop thinking about Logan and Connor and my guilt and my desire. Everything was mixed, muddled.

"Let's sleep," he said, kicking off his shoes, undoing his watch.

I watched him. Like art, he could make me move, tiny beats of my heart felt like thunder in the distance.

We crawled under the puffy white covers and he pulled me back to his chest. I couldn't do this. I couldn't sleep. I felt warmth between my thighs, my breathing was erratic.

"This isn't going to work," I said, my voice muffled into the pillow.

"What isn't?" he asked, and I pushed my ass back into him in reply. He was hard and I was thinking of all the nights I lay in bed wondering if I would ever kiss him again, ever feel him inside of me.

We shed our clothes and he entered me from behind. I cried out when he pulled on my hair, I needed this. I needed his inaudible sighs, his muffled wants.

I disconnected and turned, climbing on top of him, staring into his green eyes. What can be said without words? With only fucking and a frantic need to hold on? We made it last, then fell asleep holding each other. Before his breath turned deep and heavy, he spoke into my hair.

"You have no idea how much I've missed you."

I believed him. He missed me, but he did not love me.

LATER, we showered together, our skin had become sticky with sweat and sex.

He stepped in ahead of me. I watched him, the shower stream pouring between us, a divide. He had his eyes closed, a hair tie in his teeth.

I watched and I tasted the salt on my lips, ripped from my own eyes, as he gathered his long golden hair. His body danced and his jaw was glass. I wanted to cut myself on it.

When he was done, his locks secured on the top of his head, he opened his eyes and found mine. "What?" he asked. He could read me.

"You're the most beautiful person I've ever met."

I wasn't flirting. I couldn't say goodbye, not with the proper words, so I said this. I wanted him to remember that when I stopped taking his calls. When our friendship was no longer the last thing we clung to. I couldn't remain friends with him when I went back to Connor.

And I had decided that I would.

72

LOVE IS NEVER ENOUGH

"LOGAN ASSUMED, and it hurt him. He assumed that when I told him I would soon be off the market, I was getting into a relationship with someone new. That I would still be within his reach, easily pulled from a lover. He had done it before, maybe he assumed he could do it again."

"Could he have pulled you from someone other than Connor?"

"Of course. But he wouldn't pull me from Connor again. Love is not enough. Not by a long shot. I loved Logan but I couldn't be that girl anymore, the one who waits and wonders what's wrong with her. I got engaged to Connor on a Saturday. He bent on one knee in the living room of my trailer before a shopping trip. I wasn't surprised. We had been back together for a week. It had been two weeks since I last saw Logan. I hadn't heard from him, and I hadn't reached out. I closed doors so firmly, sometimes. I told myself that getting back with Connor would be done the right way. No more falseness, no more halfway. I knew when we got back together we would get engaged quickly. Why start from the beginning? Maybe we should have, he was a new person, and so was I."

"How did Logan take the news?"

"After announcing my engagement on Facebook, Logan deleted me as a friend. I texted him, asking why, though I knew. He said 'I can't look at that. I can't.' So I told him I was sorry and he told me not to be. He said he did this, that it was his fault."

"Did you agree with him?"

"Yes. But it still hurt to hurt him, to believe that I would never see him again. I tried to push it away, to focus on the planning and moving back in."

"Did it work?"

"For the most part. Love is never enough, is it?"

"No. You have to work at it. You have to find someone who wants to do the hard things with you."

"I believed Logan was my soulmate. But what do you do when someone is your soulmate, and you aren't theirs? My belief died with that knowledge. He made me believe in soulmates and then he made me un-believe."

"You don't believe in soulmates now?"

"No. You find someone and you love them and they love you back. You choose each other every day. On the hard days when you can't stand their voice. On the days when their face is the last thing you want to wake up to. You choose them on those days just as ardently as the days when their love is a song in your heart and you just need their arms around you. You do the work and you just don't give up. That's what I was going to do. I was going to choose Connor and I was going to do the work. Until I couldn't." The air is heavy between us, I feel myself retreating. I see my hands moving, paying a tab, leaving a tip. "I don't know how to go on. I don't know how to make this work. I can't tell it this way, not anymore."

"No?"

"No."

"Okay. Do it in a way that works. A way that works, for you and only you."

PART V

73

ONE SMALL SOLACE

THE AIR FEELS different when I land. Humid, rifling. It's spring, March, but I feel no blooming in my chest, just a hammering, a wretched need to peel my skin off so Connor can't find me.

He does though. He has no sign in his hand, nothing cheesy for his long-gone wife. We could find each other in every room, any room. I fiddle with the handle of my carry-on as I approach him, wanting to avoid his eyes.

"Let me get that," he says.

I let him, then I take the lead, but I feel a tug on my arm.

"You don't need to rush off. Look at me," he says.

I turn back, set my jaw. His eyes are sad, but not nearly as sad as the last time I saw him, when he knew I was leaving. He pulls me into a hug. I forgot how large his arms were, the way he held me full body. He speaks into my hair.

"Thanks for coming."

"Of course." I pull away and avoid his eyes again.

"Okay let's go," he says, walking ahead of me.

I always liked following him into a crowd. He knew how anxious I was when I was in a sea of people. The way I would grip his hand at the mall, on the sidewalk, at a party. He liked to make me feel safe.

HIS HOME IS INVITING, warm. I wonder who helped him decorate.

It's not the way it was when I left, warm wood walls, creams, and red. A rusty star hung on the wall above the fireplace back then. Everything now is black, white, and grey. Like my heart, like the skyline I love back in Seattle.

There is an engagement picture on the wall, our engagement picture. I'm surprised it's still up. He catches me looking at it.

I watch him cross the room, take it off the wall.

When he turns back I see the lines around his eyes. His hair has more salt and pepper beneath his ball cap.

"I just need to change and then we can head out," he says.

I nod and let him leave the room. Better for me to be alone, so I can pour over his life. Warm light spills into the living room, pulling me there. The couch is dark leather, chocolate, and smooth. I run my hand over the armrest of the loveseat. A dog runs into the room and my heart freezes. It's our youngest dog. I drop to my knees and invite him into my arms. His tail wags and he whines, I whimper in response.

When I left, I left with the cat. He kept our dogs.

Connor found me like that a few minutes later. On the floor, holding this dog. Once our dog.

No children suffered from our separation. One small solace.

SHE IS THE SEA

Connor

NOW THAT SHE was my wife, I wanted to show her my love in every way possible. Through acts of service to her. Acts of kindness. I wanted to tell her how I felt. Send her emails on the days I was at work. When she was home in a dark place, I wanted to rush home.

I wanted to show her in every way I could, how much I loved her. I took her for granted before. I thought it was enough to say I love you when she said it. I thought it was enough to put a roof over our heads, to provide monetary affections.

I was raised to only say I love you when someone was dying, when things got shitty.

I rebelled against that thinking in the beginning, like most did, when I was high off my crush on someone. Eventually, I would fade into a gentle complacency.

I did it with Gwen. I didn't appreciate her the way I should have.

Now, I wanted to show her in every damn way, that she was the end for me.

When she was leaving me, and I knew it hurt her to tell her, but I said I would never love anyone like her. I would fall for someone bright, light, alive. It wasn't what I wanted, but I tried to let her believe that.

I wanted to let her know that if she truly did leave me I would move on. I see now that I was using it as a way to emotionally manipulate her. We'd both done it, used and abused each other. But why let that past define us? I wanted to start over. I loved her more now than I ever had before. I'd seen everything inside of her that she thought was ugly, and I had seen the parts that truly were ugly.

Because no human has all good in them.

The hate she has in her heart, I want to pretend it isn't there, but it is.

I could bear it. I could bear all her hate and her ugly. I could be the shield between her and the world if she would just let me.

When she is falling, I will pull her up. That's what I'll do and it's what I am meant for.

I will move. I will travel the world. I will follow her anywhere. I have a stubborn father. I have his bones inside of me. I've broken free from the stoicism he instilled in me. I have changed.

She is worth it. Everything.

They say you shouldn't change for someone but what I have done is grow. I am a better man because of her. I am a stronger man because of her. I have new grey in my hair, in my beard. I wear it proudly.

The day she left is the day I woke up. I knew then, I needed to change my ways.

She wanted me to find a life with a new woman but there is no other woman. There is just Gwen and I love her black heart. I don't want to change it, but to ease the ache, to give her the family she never had.

Maybe it won't be the one I dreamed about, but I cannot half-ass it with a stand-in lover. I've tried and I've never felt more off, more like a liar.

I don't know how to convince her I will stay in any other way than by staying.

The act will speak for itself. Other men have given her words. Always words. False ones, not true like her writing. It's not like I've never lied to get a woman. I think most guys have. So I can't blame them completely. But any man who gets between her and me, I will wear them down. They cannot be steady like me.

I know her heart tells her settling down is boring, stale.

But I know there is an anxiousness holding onto her, that craves the stability I own. The constant, standing still.

She is the sea, the saltwater she craves.

I can be her rock. I will become any mountain, anywhere, that she needs me to be. I can give everything up for her.

75

SOMEONE LIKE YOU

WHEN I OPEN the door of the bathroom, I come face-to-face with my husband. He looks like home, like second chances.

I shake the thoughts from my head, they're just remnants, something infused into my skin, a product of our surroundings.

He's taken me to our favorite bar in downtown St. Louis.

Dinner has been broken conversation, vague searchings. I don't know what he wants from this visit, from us.

Marriage was not a fix for what ailed us. For our demons.

When I said yes to Connor, our problems did not magically float away.

My depression did not dissipate. My anxiety did not exit the room. Some days everything was amplified.

Some days I was convinced love alone could save me when deep down I knew that was a dangerous lie. It was a violent sea, being with me.

My anger became amplified at times. When Connor suggested therapy again, I raged, I rebelled.

When I finally gave in, I half-assed it. I couldn't give up my control. I wanted it in all things. I couldn't get better for him.

I had to get better for me. And even then, I wasn't ready. After two months of going just to please him, I found a strange thing happening. I looked forward to going. I quit. And then I left him.

We were married only eleven months.

CONNOR SMILES at me and I walk back to our table. I enjoy the silence while he is gone, but a voice finds its way back to me. It's in my head, a drumming.

Someone like you. It's so hard to be with *someone like you.*

It's a sentence I say over and over in my head. I practice it with different voices. The voices of different lovers who have left. Found me to be "too much".

I weigh and measure myself by standards that I do not place on others. Do I bring in enough money? Do I cook enough? Clean enough? Am I the perfect partner?

No. Definitely, not on paper, and I am in control of this paper.

It's a blurry line. Have I done this to myself or did society do this to me? Did Connor do this to me? Did his family do it to him? They gave him the perfect life, setting him up for failure, for this comparison syndrome.

When Connor returns, he stands at the table, he doesn't sit.

"What?" I ask, looking up at him. I don't like men standing over me. He knows this. There must be a strain in my eyes.

"Sorry," he says, realizing his error. He sits. "I think we should get out of here. It's too loud in here, I don't know why I thought we should talk here."

"Okay," I say, reaching for my coat and standing. I don't care where we are for this, for whatever this is.

IT WAS RAINING when we walked outside. We half ran, half walked to his car. He opened the door for me and I could hear my breathing, amplified, a chorus of fear inside.

We sat still inside, watching the rain, for five minutes, before he spoke.

"It took me a long time to find an answer to the one question you always asked: why do you love me? I never knew anyone as sad as you. I never knew someone so passionate about sticking up for people. Not just the people you knew but the people in the world. You weren't necessarily like that when I met you, but that's the woman you grew to be. Some nights during our short-lived marriage," he half laughs, we were still legally married, it wasn't over, "we would be lying in bed and you would talk for hours about the way you wanted to change the world. The way you wanted to make it fairer for everyone. My friends think you're naïve. That you don't see the world for what it is. I think they're wrong. You see the world exactly for what it is and that's why it hurts you so much."

I begin to cry, competing, losing to the rain.

"That's why you were so sad all the time. You weren't just sad about the things that happened to you. You absorbed all the hurt that the world had."

I was shaking my head, agreeing, wishing it away, I didn't know.

"When I was younger, I cared about superficial shit," he says. "On paper, you were exactly what I wanted. You are still exactly what I want but it runs deeper than your beauty. It's who you are and who you are trying to be. What can change in a year? I don't know if you still write the way you did, try the way you did, but in my mind you do. When you would ask me years ago why I loved you, I could only give you one answer."

I thought of a night on our tan sheets, fresh from the drying.

"Why do you love me?" I asked, needing something, because I could feel myself falling again, into the black.

"It's because you're real," he says those words next to me, the same words he said back then. "You were never fake. Sometimes I wished you would fake it. I wished you were better at small talk, better at socializing. But that's not you, and I spent too many years trying to put you in a box."

"You weren't as bad after we got married." My voice is small in the swelling space. His hand is on the center console, close to mine.

"Not as bad, but still doing it. It wasn't until you left that I realized all the things you hated about me were true. I was obsessed with money. But only because it meant giving you a better life than you had grown up with. I wanted to take care of you, provide for you. I wanted to have children with you and give you the children you never had."

"I stopped wanting that and you lied, you pretended you stopped wanting it, too."

"I know. My obsession with giving you the white picket fence life caused me to miss all the signs, the direct words, too. We both changed but we didn't change together. I don't know if there's anything more heartbreaking than knowing the things you want in life are no longer the same as the things the person you love wants."

I never thought I was the mothering type but he said he knew I would've been the best one. He still remembers the days in the beginning when I would smile at him and grab his hand and tell him I just wanted a little girl of my own. That was before the memories came back.

"You never gushed over babies and you never really knew how to talk to children. You talked to children like adults, but I never told you I thought that was the right way to do it. For some reason, you feel like you're doing it wrong. Everything. I've never known someone to write down their failures so intricately the way you did. Sometimes I hated the fact that you started writing."

"Trust me, I could tell. It's one reason I left."

"You were digging your own grave with it. Writing down every little flaw, dissecting it."

I cannot deny it. I like it that way. "I just picked up where you left off."

"I think you spent so many years confusing love and obsession, it was hard to separate the two."

"What was I obsessed with?" My writing, my pain. I already know the answer.

"It used to be me. Then, it wasn't."

"Your jealousy, it killed us. I learned to hate you." I did. The sound of his voice, the way he cleared his throat when he woke up in the morning. The way he whimpered in bed, at night, just wanting me to reach out to him.

"Hate and love run a lot closer to another than we want to admit. I spent a long time hating you, but I never worried that I wouldn't remember what it was like to love you. I didn't even know why I wanted you to come back here. I just wanted to look you in the eye. To tell you that you're not the only one in the world who's felt pain. That what you did to me may not be as bad as what you've been through. But it is significant. I am significant."

"I can't sit in this car with you. I can't sit here and hear this." I am frantic, I roll down the window, the rain comes in, and I push my face into it. Connor reaches for me but I push him away. "Don't touch me!" He recoils, I see his memory, his wound, open again. I screamed those words at him before. He was the one I gave my hate to. The one I punished for what my stepfather did to me.

He pulls away, reaches for the window controls on his left side. My window goes up and I stare forward, my face slick with tears and the sky's weeping.

He starts the car and we leave the parking lot.

76

IT'S ALL SHIT

WE ARRIVE at the park and I am not sure, of anything. Why I flew here, why he wanted me to.

We used to bring our dog here. We used to hold hands and lie on a blanket in the grass. I often forgot those days, the good ones. I watch Connor get out of the vehicle, his form casts shadows on the grass, then his lights go out. *His lights would have gone out if I had stayed.*

I follow him, the only thing in my hand is one notebook, the one detailing our marriage. The sound of the passenger door of his Range Rover echoes in the night.

When I reach him, he is sitting on a swing, lazily swaying forward, backward. Like we used to do.

"Tell me what it's like." He speaks to his shoes, a worn pair of boots I have seen a million times, and tried, in vain, to throw out.

"Tell you what *what* is like?"

"The sex."

"Fuck you." I halt my reach for the swing next to him. I cross my arms and feel the regret on my tongue.

"Can you just be honest with me for once? That was always your problem. You loved lying to me." He is no longer trying to convince me I am worth saving, worth wanting back. I hear it. All the things he never had the brass to ask.

"No, I just couldn't be myself with you."

"You could. You just didn't trust me enough to love you for who you were."

"And whose fault is that? Yours or mine?" I really want to know, because I don't have the answer.

"That's the question, isn't it? The one I lose sleep over. The one you gave up trying to answer."

"What was the point? Square peg, round hole." We are too different. I always said that. When I was leaving, or trying to leave, letting him convince me to stay. I still believe it.

"You always loved using that phrase on me."

"Because there is no truth I know more than that."

"What is it he gives you that I never could? Is it because he's an artist? Is it the long hair? Is it because he will hurt you in bed, the way I never could?"

"He does it because I like it. You never could because you worried too much about hurting me. And that's what killed us in the end. You never trusted me to safe out. To know my own limits." I started to want pain. To confess my desires after we got married. I told Connor I couldn't enjoy sex anymore unless I felt like I was fucking someone who didn't love me. Who didn't care to see me again. He told me he could play that game, but he didn't mean it. Not really. How could he keep up? Our sex for years was vibrant, alive. Then I woke to memories of what my stepfather did to me, and I couldn't stand to be touched at all. For years.

After we got married, I figured I could be honest with him. Vows mean no leaving, right? He couldn't leave me and all my dark? He promised not to. Logan gives me what I need because I will it, I write it.

"Those games never would have worked with me. You resented me too much."

"I didn't resent you."

"The worst part is you never just lied to me. You lied to yourself all the time. You resent me still because I pulled the truth from you. I pulled the truth from you and it made you better. It healed you in so many fucking ways and it led you to him. He gets you. That mother fucker gets the reward. I know, Gwen, I know it's been a year and I am supposed to be moving on but seeing you here now, I hate him. I hate that bastard because he stole you from me. Even when you came back, you were still his. I'm sure he is a great guy and he makes you happy but to me he is scum. He is a fucking thief."

He doesn't know how true his words are to me, to everyone. "You can't steal what's already gone."

"Nine years together and you could barely talk to me and now you're this open book. Save the truth now. It's just a goddamn knife in my gut."

"Just let me give you the divorce," I say. Isn't that what I'm here for?

"And you'll go back to your rainy day lovely life with your artist."

"Let it go." I'm so tired. So very tired of the years and the worry in my heart.

"Letting it, you, go is obviously not a skill I have learned to master. Here's the thing. I'm never going to be as broken as you. I can't win that and I don't want to. I don't want you to have been through what you've been through but I've hurt, too. You hurt me and I'm not the same man I was before. I have a darkness in me and you changed me. You never thought I could relate to you before but I can now."

"This isn't a contest." My words are biting. I feel the red I always bite down.

"Why can't you just comfort me? You never can. You're so cold. Do you comfort him?" There is more anger than blue in his voice. Sharp angles and hidden edges.

I still. "He doesn't need me to comfort him." He is more made up than man. More everything I want a lover to be.

"What does that mean?"

"He's just...content with me. We move in waves, the same direction." He is my mirror. I wrote us into existence. All that he is now, all that we were, all that we are. He is a reflection of everything I need. "With you and me, it was always back and forth. You loved me more, then I loved you more. It was never at the same time."

"So you don't hold him?"

I think of all the times Connor wanted me to touch him. To just reach my hand out, brush his temple, press my lips there. But when I felt that want from him, I froze. "You know that part of me died. It died when I found out the truth. I don't want to be held at night. I don't want a kiss on the forehead. I don't want my hand held. It wasn't just you, it's in me, this distance. This is who I am now and it had nothing to do with you."

"You weren't always like that. You loved to hold me, before."

I can barely recall those days. It's only in my notebooks that I catch glimpses of that girl. So fragile and open-hearted, even in her guarded ways. I hate that he always pulls her back up, to the surface. That he doesn't allow her to drown, as I have. "I know. And you always like to remind me of that. That I was whole once. That I was normal once."

"That's not what I meant." He speaks more openly now than I do. Less in command of his language. He lets everything out, unafraid of where it will fall.

"It doesn't matter. It's what you do to me. You take this thing that hurts me, this part of me, and you make it about you. You make it about your hurt."

"No, that's what you did to me."

I flinch at the truth. "I just wanted to be left alone! I wanted to be left alone and you wouldn't go away. You made it about you. Like, something had been stolen from you, not me. That my change had ruined your future! You were selfish. You wanted me to stay with you so you could be happy. You didn't care that I was dying. Trying to be normal and happy and perfect for you. The little suburban housewife. The perfect little woman just like your mother and sister. You stopped seeing what I wanted. If I had never left, would you have let me go so I could be happy? Or would you have watched me wither away in front of you? Watched me change everything about myself so I could be what you wanted?" I think he would have.

"I wanted you to be happy. That's why I wanted you to go to therapy."

And here we are, transported back in time. "You wanted me to go to therapy so I could be better FOR YOU!"

"Why do you always say that?"

I say it because he does not listen. So many years of jokes about my short attention span. About the way I never listened to what he said, and he was doing it, too. "Because that's how it felt. One more thing to cross off your list for your cookie cutter life."

"I just wanted us to be happy." He looks down at his boots again.

"Well, we weren't. You would have lived the rest of your life miserable with me. You would have taken that over being happy."

"Happy the way I am now? I've had you and I haven't had you. It's worse without you."

"If it were right, you would say it was right with me and without me it was wrong. Instead, you're saying without me it's wrong and with me it's a little less wrong. We are both still young-ish. You struck out with me, but there's someone out there who will make you wish you had never met me."

"Most days I do wish I had never met you. I was happy, healthy, before you."

"And that's not what love is."

"Love is pain, sacrifice."

"It has to be more than that." I'm not sure what it is, but there must be more.

"Do you have that now?"

"Close enough. It's not in the cards for me, that perfect thing. The kind you think exists."

"What about your version of perfect?"

I laugh, no song there, no smile in my eyes. "I have no version of perfect. It's all shit."

77

MY PERFECT LIE

I WONDER if Connor would have had enough warmth to sustain all of us. Me and a child and himself. He is stronger than I could ever imagine, more in tune with his heart, so changed and grown up. I look back at the cold years of our relationship when we were more like roommates than lovers.

He told me he would get off in the shower, and that was fine. I would get off under the covers after he left for work.

We couldn't find anything in each other worth desiring. I hate telling people that, writing it.

I kept the secrets of us, our relationship and our marriage, under wraps. Best not to let anyone see the cracks, the fissures.

I live my life like a beautiful painting, a beautiful lie. I put the pretty on social media, hide the ugliest of truths.

What good is all of this thick skin if all I do is hide from the world? Can't I walk into the sunlight and hold my head high? Mean it when I say that I don't care what other people think of me? Put my money where my mouth is?

I look at Connor's hands on the chain of the swing. I need Connor to hold my hand. I am not too proud to feel that.

He was a crutch, a warm place to land and it's so strange to me that we can go through so many waves, so many changes, with another soul.

So many truths and questions have been answered here in the dark, in this park.

We are not what we once were and our history is riddled with lies, deceit.

"Are you ready to tell the truth?" he asks me, because he knows I am. He knows why I came here, why I confess, why I write. He knows even when I tell him he doesn't. My rage and rebellion from love can't change his truth.

"How do we make this clean now? How do we make this our own version of perfect?" I want to be the wife I always hoped I would be. With him, the constant, unwavering husband I never thought I would get. The other men who got close, they wouldn't be able to hold me the way he does. Hold me up and keep me from drowning. One of the hardest things to live through is knowing someone doesn't want you anymore after you've shown them every ugly crack in your soul. Avery, years ago, saw mine and left me. Logan saw them and lied the way I lied. I was young and foolish then, to think I could spend my lives with them. Maybe that's why I cringe when young people say they want to get married. I want them to get out there and live their lives. To take the time and care to find someone who will change with them. I know it happens early for some, but it didn't for me. I was a different woman then and we couldn't have grown together, those men and I. I was twenty-five when I met Connor and still so raw and unlearned, so foolish and naïve about the world. I have never seen someone transform themselves completely.

Maybe I can? I have I guess, just not in the right direction.

I've regressed since I learned about my abuse. I opened up and I told the world, yet it placed more bars on my heart. Each level of secrets revealed has built more walls. I was failing. That's why I have to tell it this way.

I look down at my hand, at the truth. "I brought everything here. The pictures and the notebooks and this pain in my chest. I want to bury it, to burn it, for you to take it, I don't care. Whatever you think is best. Whatever you want me to do with it, I'll do it."

He finally stands, moved by the change in my voice. He knows what it means. He knows me.

"I want to move on from this, from this beginning and ending and the middle. All of it." My voice cracks and I clench my eyes. Everything is gone, the things I made up and the lies. Logan, my *perfect* life, my perfect lie. "I want to know something beautiful can grow from this. That opening up doesn't have to be the end of everything. That someone will see all of this ugly in me, and tell me where the beauty is."

When he reaches me, he kisses me like he means it, and he always has. Even when he hated me, he kissed me with the kind of honesty I let die in my throat.

He is beauty and life and I am alive because he believes in me, for some reason.

The fairytales don't compare to the work he does. To the day in and the day out.

He endures.

My love is poison. His kisses are mine. They always have been. He doesn't steal life from me, he breathes it back into me.

How does anyone survive without this kind of love? How does he see me the same way, every day? I know he loved me even when he hated me. Even when I was killing him. When I left him. When I lost myself. We're more than this story or the way people see it. When he pulls away, he stares into my eyes. He always said they looked nearly black in the night, my dark blue melted away.

"I'll pick you up when you're done."

I feel a dissolve, the slow melt of my story, our story. I blink and I am not alone, I am looking into warm eyes.

78

EXHUME

I STARE AT MY PHONE. The vibration has pulled me from the story.

Connor: I'll pick you up when you're done.

"Sorry," I say, looking at the clock on the wall, and she follows my eyes. I take another drink. It's water, not the clear poison I wanted for this.

"Yes. Our time today is almost up." The illusion is gone. The airport is gone. It's as it is. A room of creams and whites. I do not sit on the couch, this hasn't been the cliché I worked it up to be, back when I rejected it all.

"It always goes this way. Time slips by too quickly." I start to gather my things, my therapist's words still me.

"Will you write it differently? How much truth is in that story?"

"A lot, a lot of lies, too."

"I think that's just called fiction, no?"

"Yes," I pause, "fiction."

"Was Logan real?"

We will rehash this, go back to the beginning. I hope I'm ready then. "Yes. For a fleeting moment."

"Do you know where Logan is these days?"

"No." And it's the truth. I had to exhume him for his, but I will bury him again.

"Do you ever think about him?"

"Rarely. What once burned so brightly in my heart, died out. I thought he would always be close to my mind. But he isn't." It hurts to know that love can fade so fully. "It's only when I hear his name, or see someone who looks like him. When I remember him, it is a dull ache. A sadness at what could have been, of what I would have eventually run from. You cannot love a lie, and a liar, as fully as you hope to. He was more a phantom than a man. I hope he is still lying. So I'll always know I was right about him."

"Is that a healthy way to look back at it?"

"No. But that's why I come here, right? To fix myself?" I clutch my purse in my lap.

"Was Penny real?"

"In the beginning. She didn't last in our lives past that summer."

"So there was no other woman?"

"No, it was always me for him. Always."

"Then why write her into the story in that way?"

"I needed someone else to blame. Someone other than myself. I needed a villain. I couldn't let it be me. I couldn't face that."

"You see the truth in your tale though, right? In the end, he wanted you. The same way he wants you now, the same way he chooses you every day. Why write yourself apart?"

"I guess I don't know him any other way. I only know him searching for me, reaching for me as I pull."

"Why did you put yourself with Logan?"

"Because I wouldn't have been happy with him. I wrote me running back to Connor because that's what I'll always do. I wrote me betraying both, because that's what I did. I had to punish myself."

"I hope you know, what matters now, is what you choose to do going forward. Do you think you'll leave and betray Connor again?"

"Never. I'll never do that again."

"Then you need to stop punishing yourself. The past is done, over. We can only learn from it. Move forward and choose more wisely with the information we have gathered from all we have done and all the ways we have stumbled."

"How do I break the cycle? How do I stop nailing myself to the cross?"

"That's why we're here, now. To talk it out. To let our wounds breathe and heal."

"I've always been a walking wound. I can see why people sometimes choose to just fade away. It's easier than facing all we have done and all we have hurt. I wanted to do that, for so many years. Connor even said he felt that way once. I made the smiling, laughing man cry, I made him wish he wasn't alive. I don't understand it. He has more forgiveness in him than anyone I know."

"He chose you. You wrote it yourself. If you choose him back, like you say you do, it's time to accept the fact that you can be happy. That the past doesn't matter. You were not given a dark mark when you were a child. You can rise above and have the life you want."

I look into her eyes, feel more stretching, more bricks falling.

"What's more important than him choosing you though," she stands, I mirror her, "is that you choose yourself."

79

LIKE I MEAN IT

When I walk out into the spring March air, I shiver.

I see my husband standing outside, talking on the phone. He ends the conversation as I walk to him.

He opens his arms and pulls me into a hug. I want to cry, so I do. I don't hide my heart with as much vehemence, not as I used to. It's still black and bloody, but we are healing it.

I have been going to therapy for a year. I started after I tried to leave him before our first wedding anniversary. I thought marriage could fix me, but that's not the way the world works.

My red rage has lessened in ways I never knew it could. It is not perfect, this life we have, not by a long shot, but I am climbing out of this hole.

A pink letter falls out of the notebook tucked under my arm. It blows in the wind and Connor catches it by stepping on it. He dusts it off and smiles at me when he comes back to me.

"This old letter. Damn."

Three years ago, when I left Connor, he sent me flowers every Wednesday for a month. Finally, I had to tell him to stop. To let him know the flowers hurt me. It was a reminder of how I broke us. His last delivery of roses had a letter stuffed inside the envelope. The small white thing bulged with the words.

Connor starts reading the letter in front of me, he turns so I can follow along.

Gwen,

Wow, what a crazy couple of weeks we have had. For that matter, what a crazy seven years since we met. We've had ups, we've had downs, we've been through so fucking much together. Memories I will cherish forever.
Firstly, I want you to know my silence toward you over the next few months is not me ignoring you and I hope it will not come across as disinterest, it's exactly the opposite. I love you so much and whether it's with me or without me, I truly want you to be happy in life. If a clean break and solid time apart is what you need to feel happy right now, then I am going to give you that. I'm going to listen to you and respect your wishes. I don't want to smother you like I did before you moved out. I'm sorry for that. I just wanted to spend all the time I could with you before you left. I think this letter and giving you space is the only way I can show you that I realize if you gave me another chance it would be different for us and I would be committed to changing the things you need from me and would need from me in the future.
Like showing you more love and passion. I would shout my love for you in front of everyone. I know I didn't react the way I should have in the past, but this is different. I am different. I didn't express my feelings properly before, I was a stupid guy who didn't fully understand himself. It took the love of my life, you, breaking up with me to realize that you are the one I always wanted to spend the rest of my life with and that I need to grow up and change if I want that to happen.
I have done a lot of self-reflection and there is so much I need to work on. A great relationship is a partnership. I want us both to feel comfortable communicating and expressing what we want from each other.
Five years is a long time and if not as my lover, I need you as my friend. My life without you is not the life I want and I am so sorry you've had to wait until this point for me to grasp this.
I can't help but remember all the times at Paul's Wingstop, the times we had in your trailer, or even the years in the house we shared.

I can't believe how lucky I got that it was my car you left your purse in. Every time I have thought of our past over these last few weeks, it has brought a smile to my face. I want to go back to those times. I want us to enjoy ourselves again like we used to. When we never let what other people thought of us stand in our way. Maybe we can't go back to that, or should, but I would love the chance to carve out a new life with you.

We could create our own life together on our terms. No white picket fence or what others think we should have. Kids or no kids. Adopting or having one of our own. Whatever you want is what I want.

I am so proud of you and your writing and I know you will go far. I am always here if you want to tell me how it's going, what is happening. My phone will always welcome a call from you. Even if it's just to talk or blow off steam. I will always be here for you.

I am here waiting, and I always will be.

I wish you the best and I hope, one day, I can be a part of your life again.

Connor

WHEN WE ARE DONE READING, he folds the letter up. I have a tear in my eye. That damn purse I left in his car brought it out of me. Seeing again, that he knew we were meant to find each other too, makes me ache.

I want to say we found a happily ever after. That I gave him the children he wanted. That I let him love me fully every day. But I can't do that. I can't let good in all the way, not yet.

I will rebel against it until I die. I will rebel and I will be me, ugly and torn. I can't be less.

When I look back at us, I see me being less. I see me trying to be good, pure, quiet, and meek. Less sloppy, less slutty, less mentally broken. I see me being all those fake things on the surface so I can make everyone happy.

I want to write an ending for everyone that is neat but I am not neat. I am not happily-ever-after. I am if I lie, and I am so tired of lying.

What if I just say we are trying? That we are trying to work through this. To be better, for each other.

Is it a lie if some days I do not feel it in my heart? If I just want to leave him for good so he can have all he wants? I will always be a runner, but my love can be found in the places he pulls it from.

He takes the journal from under my arm and tucks the letter inside, then he sets it on the hood of our car and pulls me in for a hug. I like the weight of him, the way he feels. "How was it today?" he asks the question to my long brown hair.

"Better. We ended the story." I pull away and look into his dark eyes, run my hand along his stubble.

"So what now?"

I run my hand along his arm, pushing up the sleeve of his shirt. He has a tattoo there of a woman with stitched lips. A representation of who I used to be. Stitched lips and confessions locked tight. They slip out now, in poetry and on paper, to him, to my therapist.

"We start at the beginning again. I tell it again, but with no lies. No fiction."

"And what about us?"

I kiss him. I kiss him like I mean it. Like our vows and our hearts and our scars and our imperfect love, our imperfect life.

"We start at the beginning."

ACKNOWLEDGMENTS

Thank you to my family and friends. Thank you for understanding how important this career is, and sacrificing time with me so I can hide in my office.

Thank you to all of the bloggers. Your love of books and endless devotion is so important. I would be lost without you all.

My Rebels, *thank you thank you thank you.* Our group is a lifeline. I hope you all stay around after you've seen the real me in this book.

Kat, thank you for always being a true friend. I am so proud of you and the direction your writing is going. You're going to kill it.

Christina, I have no idea what to say. You've held my hand through all of this. I appreciate all of the encouragement, the scary flowers, and the way you ALWAYS believe in me.

Cody, what is this life? People are going to read this and think we are the worst couple ever. But, we've never listened to anyone before, right? Why start now?

ABOUT THE AUTHOR

J.R. Rogue first put pen to paper at the age of fifteen after developing an unrequited High School crush & has never stopped writing about heartache.

She has published multiple volumes of poetry such as Tell Me Where It Hurts, All Of My Bullshit Truths & Exits, Desires, & Slow Fires, & two other novels, Burning Muses & Background Music.

J.R. ROGUE is very active on social media & encourages you to follow her around.

www.jrrogue.com
contact@jrrogue.com

ALSO BY J. R. ROGUE

Novels

Burning Muses

Background Music

Poetry

La Douleur Exquise

Tell Me Where It Hurts

An Open Suitcase & New Blue Tears

Rouge

Le Chant Des Sirènes

Letters to the Moon

All Of My Bullshit Truths: Collected Poems

Exits, Desires, & Slow Fires

Made in the USA
Columbia, SC
01 August 2019